CURSE
OF
THE
CHINDI

BY SANDRA FENDLER

In Memory of My Beloved Brother
My dear brother gave his family and friends the gift of his presence.
Preserved in this book is his memory ~ to be kept alive and treasured forever.

ACKNOWLEDGEMENTS

This book is published in tribute to my family and friends. A special thanks goes to my two sons who gave me the inspiration and determination to write this novel. I also wish to thank my long-time friends, Dana, Kathy and Marilyn, for their input and support. I sincerely appreciate the guidance and assistance with the final stages of the manuscript provided by Pat Richmond and Carol Osman Brown.

You obviously came into my life for a purpose. You know we are all connected.

FOREWARD

My brother Clayton, entrepreneur of the family, had successfully initiated and developed several business establishments in central and northern Arizona. He invited Mother and me to visit his latest venture—a century-old trading post compound that he had bought, restored, and now was operating in the heart of the Navajo Reservation. Mid-August and the late arrival of the summer monsoon season made us delighted to have an opportunity to escape the *Valley of the Sun's* sizzling one hundred sixteen-degree heat. Mother and I looked forward to an enjoyable and relaxing trip, although we knew all about the monsoon season's awesome thunderstorms, torrential rains, and flash-flooding in arroyos. Those hazards would become the least of our worries. We had planned our trip thoroughly, but no plan could foresee or take into account the horrors of forthcoming encounters with the Navajo spiritual world that included the fearsome *Chindi*.

Sarah Simms

CHAPTER I

If you're in a hurry, even the shortest and fastest route between Phoenix and the heart of Navajo land in the mountainous terrain of northern Arizona, with its flat-topped mesas and dramatically shaped spires, means a four hundred-mile, eight-hour drive.

Nothing was in bloom in the shimmering summer heat. Spring had dutifully produced its abundance of blue lupine, mariposa lilies, wild varieties of colorful poppies, and the unique brittlebush with its bright yellow flowers bursting their showy display of color. But now, even the ocotillo cactus that had bloomed a bright red after summer's first rain was stoically suffering the sun's rays.

It was such a gawd-awful hot day in the sprawling metropolitan Valley of the Sun. Looking forward to this much-needed respite, I was glad we had taken my brother up on his offer to see his trading post.

"I hope you battened everything down before we left," I said to Mother, breaking the silence. "Another storm is moving in. They're expecting torrential rain and forty-mile per hour winds."

Summer is our season for the monsoons, when southerly winds send black clouds across the desert to darken the late afternoons. You can almost set your watch by the first clap of thunder at 4 p.m.

"Speaking of weather, Sarah, I hope you brought something warm to wear. It's predicted to dip to the low 40s." She looked at me with a maternal concern in her soft blue eyes.

"Yes, Mother," I sighed. "Of course I brought suitable clothes for the high country." I glanced at my Louis Vuitton bags, methodically packed and ready for any exciting venture that might come my way. "You know I don't travel light!"

I never gave much thought to how much I counted on my mother. The reverse always seemed true. In fact, all the family members generally looked to me to be responsible for family concerns. But she, in her cheerful, positive way, was the one who inspired and motivated me. She was really the heart and source of my strength in the trials ahead.

As we continued northward, long rows of saguaros, their trunks and arms reaching twenty feet into the air, covered the rugged, undulating hills, sentinelling the meadow below. The road wound higher into the foothills, where a few persistent saguaro cacti still lingered on the landscape, looking as if they might have been returning from a scouting expedition.

Approaching the first stop light in Payson, we saw the sign stating, "Welcome to Payson, the Rodeo Capital of Arizona!" and realized we were hungry. We drove past the blacksmith shop on Old Main Street, pulled into the parking lot of the old-time saloon known as the Oxbow Inn, and walked through the familiar covered entranceway past the hitching posts, to the two large wooden doors. We seated ourselves at a table next to the paned glass window that looks out at Old Main Street, where the historic rodeos called the "August Doin's" were held before the new arena was built. Throughout our lunch of chicken fried steak, Mother displayed the elation she felt. Her mood was euphoric because she was going to visit her son.

In my mother's eyes, Clayton, was always the "sweet angel" who could do no wrong. I was the "mischievous imp," who could do no right. She never caught on that he was the one who always got me into trouble. Even as a little boy, he had an uncanny way of teasing, but not in a malicious way. He did so with such a childlike innocence that he ultimately forced me to laugh at myself.

Visiting Payson always reminded me of the adventures I shared with my brother, mother, and my two sons during our stays at the family cabin in the woods. Those were wonderful times, I thought, remembering the incredible peace that rose from within as I relaxed on the deck of the multi-level structure, its knotty-pine floor cantilevered over a bubbling creek.

"There are times when I miss our little cabin by the creek and this Rim Country," I sighed to Mother.

I fondly recalled trekking through the Rim Country with my camera, photographing the flowers, buildings, and people that made this such a colorful part of Arizona.

We bought the cabin so we could be near a tall stand of Ponderosa pine trees. The trees rose from down by the creek to tower over the house. That's where Clayton and I saw the bear tracks one year. Very early one spring, while the weather was still chilly, I had decided it would be a good day to go hiking. Naturally, I wanted my brother to go with me. It was not yet dawn when we went quietly down the back stairs, Clayton carrying the flashlight ahead of me as I fumbled with my camera. We took the covered walkway around to the side of the house. I stopped, momentarily frozen with shock. I gasped and then whispered, "Oh, my gosh, what made those tracks—a dinosaur?"

"Well, if I were you, I'd play it safe and stay indoors this season. Those are bear tracks," Clayton advised. "Either that or wear your mink coat. They might mistake you for a distant relative!" Clayton always found humor in everything. I only thought about how I'd like to get a picture of a real bear.

Midway between our cabin and the neighbor's was a dry wash, and to the right there was a seldom-used hiking trail where Clayton and I had seen a mountain lion the previous year. That same day, we had spotted an elk basking in the sun on a nearby ridge. Over our many years of vacationing there we had also seen red fox, deer, javelina and bobcat, but never a bear. We continued to follow the bear prints as they crossed under a stretch of fence line, until we came upon a gently rolling hillside. Just as I was beginning to give up hope of any pictures, we saw the bear.

"Get a little closer," I said, as I focused my camera.

"If I get any closer, I'm going to end up being the bear's dinner!"

"Nonsense, Clayton!" I laughed.

"Smile!" I clicked the camera.

I looked up in time to see my brother sprint past me, arms flailing in every direction.

"You'd better put a little spring in your step, Sarah," Clayton quipped as he passed. That's when I saw the bear charging toward us. The rumbling sound in his throat sounded like a train. What a fright! Like Jack and Jill, we came tumbling down the hill, the bear trailing behind us. He stopped as we ducked under the fence.

Safely back at the cabin, Clayton turned to me. "They say wisdom comes from experience. What do you think we learned today, Sarah?"

"That we're really stupid!"

My brother threw me a disdainful look. "Now can we go back to sleep?"

"Whenever we come up to the Rim country, it seems that I miss the cabin all the more," I said to Mother, as we paid for our lunch. "Nothing's the same anymore."

"You know, I really regret you having to sell that place," Mother said with sympathy in her voice. "Are we still going to stop by and see it?"

I replied, "We sure are!"

As we drove through the cool pines, I caught sight of two little boys, their fishing poles slung over their shoulders and kerchiefs poking out of their back pockets. They were heading to the creek. It reminded me of when my sons were that age. Was it almost ten years ago when our family used to romp and play in the Rim country? Where does the time go?

Back then, Tonto Creek was a playground for my two sons, Preston and Conner, who were inseparable from their loyal canine pal, Gucci, a massive boxer with an impressive pedigree. My little sons were as eager and excited as the brindle boxer dog leaping after them. Together, they hiked through the bushes and cottonwoods that grew like an oasis along the creek's banks. They loved cascading down with the water, spilling from a rock overhang, splashing into the foamy catchment below. As we approached our old cabin, my mind was adrift, pleasantly remembering the fun we used to have. I parked the car in front of the driveway. Rather than attempting to trespass on property that no longer belonged to us, we sat in the car and quietly admired the cabin. I looked at Mother.

She said, "My, my. It looks just like it used to. It's had good care."

Wherever you go in the Rim Country, many unique natural wonders lie just off the highway, hidden from all except those who take the time to explore. One such offering is the Tonto Natural Bridge, which is thought to be the world's largest travertine bridge. The one hundred eighty-three-foot-high bridge is one hundred fifty feet wide inside and shelters a four hundred-foot-long tunnel. For hundreds of years, the Tonto Apaches used it as a seasonal camp.

Clayton once told me that he actually stumbled upon the secret stronghold of Geronimo and his band of renegades not far from here. He was a walking encyclopedia on the best wilderness walks for history buffs. "The Highline Trail was known in the 1880s as the link between homesteads and ranches strung out just beneath the Rim," he told us, "but actually had been a game trail for a couple of thousand years before that. It's kind of neat, too, to know that Zane Grey used to hike and ride that same ground."

The Mogollon Rim, one of the most impressive sights north of Payson, rises to a height of more than 7,000 feet. Its massive 2,000-foot escarpment was now visible in our car window. Four wide lanes alternated back and forth between two-lane highways as we traveled north into the high country, leaving the Payson area and its memories behind. It all seemed so wonderful. How was I to know what was to come?

Hypnotized by the yellow line and the steady speed, I was caught unaware when the terrain changed dramatically. I found myself looking at the scruffy vegetation most characteristic of the high, arid desert that peppered the enormous stretches of flatlands. Almost in defiance of nature, the scrubby-looking plants sprouted through the dry wrinkled skin of the desert floor.

Dark clouds were forming over the Navajo Reservation, threatening to descend over the mountains as Mother and I stretched back in our seats. Intent on arriving at the trading post before dark, we kept looking for the turnoff, supposedly a signpost the size of a huge billboard that would lead us to the reservation. Lost in nostalgia, my thoughts drifted back in time, encouraging me to contemplate the lives of the people who lived there. Just as I was about to capture the feeling of what life must have been like hundreds of years ago, I was startled, my tranquility interrupted as I heard Mother.

"Stop, Sarah!" she shouted, her voice a piercing shrill. "You just missed the McGinnis signpost!"

Without warning, we had inadvertently passed our turnoff. Finding a dusty rut off the road and turning around, I had the feeling that we were turning back in time, traveling into a lost era. The old McGinnis sign, as described by Clayton, was worn with time, reminiscent of days gone by. An arrow pointed to the otherwise unmarked road. Breathing a sigh of relief, a frightening thought occurred to me. What if he isn't there to meet us? I felt a shiver of anxiety, knowing how unpredictable Clayton could be, one of the imperfections that makes him unique. For the next five miles, Mother and I drove through the outlying areas of the reservation. Some of the roads were unmarked, and the Feldman Gas Station described by my brother as another guidepost never seemed to materialize.

"Maybe we should pull in there," Mother suggested, interrupting my thoughts. "It's the only building that we've seen for the last five miles. And, it *is* on the left—like Clayton said."

Pulling the car to a stop with its engine still idling, I stared in disbelief. This can't be it. I glanced at the old-looking stone-faced building with its antique gas pumps. "This place looks like it hasn't been occupied for fifty years. It is certainly the 'old-time gas station' that Clayton talked about," I said, but he neglected to mention it had been abandoned. Well, so much for filling the gas tank. Let's hope we can make it to the trading post."

Shaking my head, I smiled to myself, as Mother began to laugh. The tinkling sound of her laughter reminded me of a succession of notes played in a high octave on the piano keys. Perhaps the fact that she was an accomplished musician who still gave piano lessons was the reason the analogy came to mind.

We impulsively turned onto the unfamiliar, unmarked, and unpaved road. It was the beginning of a rutted, washboard track that went on endlessly, eventually climbing upward.

"There are lots of hills," I breathed in exasperation. "Which one do you suppose he meant?" I asked, although I didn't expect a response. Seeing a fork in the road, I turned. "I hope this is the right way," I said, as we followed the contour, hugging the narrow ridgeline.

We approached a thick stand of Tamarisk trees and saw the silhouette of a small structure. Standing in front was a pretty little Indian girl dressed in the traditional Navajo custom, an ornament fastened to her thick, dark braid. As she turned to face us, her expression was one of acceptance, pleased to see someone in this obscure region. She approached the car with happy abandon, as if she were expecting us.

"Do you know where the Blue Sage Trading Post is?" I asked, deliberately enunciating each syllable.

Without a word, she stared at me, raised her arm, and pointed to the distant mountain.

We began driving through the reservation with its long valleys and flat-topped mesas. In general, the land is arid and high, ranging from three thousand feet above sea level to nine thousand feet in the mountains, in the center and west of the reservation. With the exception of the pine-covered mountain ranges, precipitation seldom exceeds ten inches a year, and in many places it is considerably less. At one point, in the middle of the vast barrenness we came upon a plain, rectangular building. I was shocked at what I saw. Paint cans, rusted bed springs, and cast-off appliances were strewn haphazardly all over the yard of an old wooden building, like scars on the stark landscape. On the periphery, an old broken-down truck, with its paint peeled and scraped, remained parked on its rims, discarded parts piled in a heap beside it.

I was appalled and bewildered by the anomaly. Even though I admired what they have preserved and with what fortitude they've preserved it, I puzzled over how a people who so adamantly uphold their legacy in the old Navajo way of living could leave their own yards in such a state. I fantasized about a long ago culture and life revolving around day-to-day necessities and survival. Lost in thought, I pondered…change happens in every culture. What would this have looked like before the white man came? There would have been no washing machines and broken-down trucks. Are the Indian tribes better off now? Are we? Sometimes I wonder if we are any happier with all our modern conveniences. Deep inside, do we all long for something simple and untouched from the past?

I continued to traverse the long, endless road surrounded by this vast and desolate land. While gazing at the monotonous landscape, thinking of how I loved searching for unspoiled environments and finding undiscovered pockets of indigenous cultures, another curious sight appeared. Next to an old farmhouse was a conical-shaped dwelling, completely covered with skins. I couldn't believe my eyes. It was a real, honest to goodness tepee, with its frame of sticks protruding through the opening at the top. Like a set transplanted from a Western movie, this enclave was complete, not only with its own tepee, but also with an authentic Navajo-made hogan. Characteristic of the mud and log hexagonal structure, the door of the hogan was traditionally facing east.

Immense sandstone cliffs began to unfold, tier upon tier, revealing the extent of their stark, ageless beauty. Altars made of stone seemed to swell from the flesh of the earth; mystical towers and turrets were crowned overhead by a nearby butte. With bare, creamy rock enveloping us, it seemed we were entering a secret celestial gateway framed by the sheer faces of the sandstone walls. Jagged mountains with cathedral-like spires thrust into the sky in virtual insurrection.

The road twisted and with each turn my anxiety rose. I was exhausted. Our energy and fuel were practically depleted. I wondered if we were ever going to reach the top. Glancing upward at the mountains' crests with their serrated peaks almost piercing the clouds, we continued ascending, spiraling our way up…and up. Blinding white sand, sand the color of fine-textured alabaster, stretched out before us as we finally reached the crest. Then, suddenly, the trading post appeared, like a bird's nest perched atop a rock outcropping, a pedestal rock supporting its massive foundation.

The trading post was unprotected except by a mountain to the east. The overhanging face of rock was like a shroud, sheltering it from obscurity and empty desolation. Unlike the mountains that remained practically untouched by the ravages of time, the trading post, with its cluster of long, low buildings looked antiquated, conveying the spirit of a frontier mystique. But we were to learn that, like a wolf in sheep's clothing, its true identity was masked.

As shadows lengthened across the barren high desert mesas, I could see the skeletal blades of a windmill. With the sun's rays striking off the tips and shining with a lurid red glow, it had a menacing feeling. The day's light was fading and the overcast sky promised a moonless night. There was a faint copper tint to the air and the smell of dust from the August drought filled our senses.

Grim quiet greeted us as we stood at the entry. In finding one of the doors unlocked, and after peeking around it, I took a step inside. Forcing myself to move forward, I took a step farther, breathing in the dank smell of moist earth. It was dim and silent inside the trading post's creaky old house. I felt an underlying sense of uneasiness.

"Hello, anybody home? Where are you? Clayton?" My voice disappeared into silence as the walls absorbed it. "This is preposterous! Where is he? We're not even certain if we have the right place," I said, glancing at Mother.

Confused, I stood back against the far wall and suddenly my expression lightened.

"This has to be Clayton's house," I said, looking at the stacks of unpacked boxes and miscellaneous junk. Piled high, the clutter filled the corner of the vacant room. "Just look at all this mess."

Mother attempted to stifle a laugh and then laughed again, this time the pitch a bit higher.

"I fail to see the humor in this," I grumbled. "Not only that, but this place gives me the creeps."

Mother moved closer to me. Hastily retracing our steps, we retreated to the outside. Unfolding two of the lawn chairs that were stacked by the door, we sat, waiting for Clayton. A strange hush came over the top of the summit, making it possible to hear the harmonious howls of the coyotes, pulsating up from the valley floor. The palpable wildness of their sounds, swaddled in an echo, made them seem threatening as darkness gradually closed around us.

With the sun's descent below the mountain, the air became very cold. I pulled my sweatshirt down over my knees, tucking my chin in its collar. Slightly shivering, I was unconvinced by Mother's suggestion to go inside. With my personal dreams of escaping city life, I was determined to remain outside and indulge in the nostalgia of living in simpler times. This place, sitting on top of the world, was like being in the last frontier outpost of the West.

Suddenly, a chilling, oddly rhythmical wind began to surround us. In the corner of the house, I could see the grotesquely shaped interlocking branches of the Juniper tree that had begun scraping on the metal eaves of the roof. As the century-old tree began to sway, a flurry of frantic commotion erupted. With a whirring of wings, something moved through it, fanning in all directions. Several little furry creatures flew past my head. Disquieted by the intrusion of the bats, I stood up, anticipating something even more unfavorable. "Perhaps we had better go inside," I suggested apprehensively.

There was something terribly compelling about this place. It was so quiet, with an almost unhealthy stillness. I could feel it all around me, following me, as we made our way through the arteries extending into the chambers of the rambling house. Just as we turned to go into what appeared to be Clayton's bedroom, I heard a sound. I froze as I glimpsed a fleeting black shadow of a male figure disappearing into the gloom. Where did he go? I cringed. Mother and I rushed into the bedroom. I walked over to the window like a frightened child, hoping not to encounter the dreaded, legendary *Chindi* of Navajo lore.

Into the stillness came the sounds, unrecognizable sounds that sent prickles of electricity all down my spine. My face pressed against the glass. My eyes wide and fixed, I peered through the bedroom window. Staring out, my gaze focused on the black-on-black shadow at the corner of the house from where the unintelligible cries were coming. Seeing nothing, my foreboding grew.

"Mother? Don't you hear that?" But my words were drowned by the anguished cries. Mesmerized by its energy, I stood motionless, trembling with tension and fright. "Mother? Don't you hear that?" I repeated, sharply. But a blank expression and sense of doubt was reflected in my mother's eyes as she sat on the bed. By then, the ominous sounds were fading, becoming a thin wail. As intermittently as they came, they disappeared, one by one, as if being swallowed by the dark.

I slipped out of the bedroom into darkness. As my eyes adjusted to night vision, I groped for the light. Sufficiently able to see, I proceeded to thread my way through the maze of rooms, my anxiety and fear mounting. I found myself at the entrance of a huge, cavernous chamber stocked with everything imaginable. Stopping short, I assessed the room. Everywhere, the walls were lined with racks and shelves stacked with food and supplies. Propped against the wall next to a new galvanized washtub was a metal rod about four feet in height and three inches in diameter. This would make a good weapon, I thought, as I turned to go back. Grabbing it with an almost primal instinct and hugging it to me, I retreated. Reaching the safety of the bedroom, I closed the door behind me. It had no lock. Propping my rod against the door, I breathed a sigh of consternation. Was this really happening? In trying to separate truth from fantasy, I could no longer be sure.

"Where is Clayton?" I said aloud, my exasperation beyond words. "He should have been here by now."

As an endless blur of time passed, I became simultaneously angered and worried. Assessing the situation and feeling no imminent danger, I opened the door. The adjacent room had been made into a makeshift office, exhibiting a kind of unpremeditated decor. In front of a tall metal file cabinet was an old wooden desk, its top scratched and scarred with the abuses of time, a phone nestled in the clutter.

Taking a deep breath and saying a quick prayer, I dialed Clayton's other business, some three hundred miles away. "He had better not be there," I remarked, noticeably agitated. It was now ten p.m. and if he weren't already on his way, he wouldn't start at this late hour.

A voice on the other end of the line finally answered. "Cornflower Corners Saloon and Steakhouse." It was Clayton, his usual carefree voice revealing his basic tendency to live-and-let live.

"Where are you?" I demanded. But before he could answer, I tried to explain what had just happened, not fully comprehending it myself.

Tauntingly, Clayton casually remarked, "Don't worry, Sarah; it's just the *Chindi*." His voice was a soft whisper.

"What do you mean, 'It's just the *Chindi*?'" I shot back at him. "I don't need to hear about your damned *Chindi* right now, Clayton!"

"I'm serious, Sarah."

"Yeah, right!" I pictured his perverse smile.

"The local inhabitants believe that the trading post is haunted by the curse of the *Chindi*, Navajo evil spirits or supreme evil, comparable to our devil," he whispered dramatically. "It's the malevolent ghosts of the dead, the *Chindi*, who have disrupted the balance of good harmony.

Having gained the terrible powers of witchcraft, they have returned seeking revenge," he breathed hoarsely, his vocal cords vibrating in a lower pitch.

Realizing that my younger brother had done little to comfort me with his peculiar distorted sense of humor, and knowing he wouldn't be making the long trip this night, I angrily hung up on his laughing promise to arrive the following morning. Would he never grow up?!

"This is beginning to have every earmark of a disastrous vacation," I grumbled, as I cautiously made my way back to the bedroom and found Mother already in bed and asleep. Soundlessly, I undressed. Sitting on the edge of the bed, the memory of the unearthly sounds rang in my ears, almost too loud to endure, yet too soft to grasp. I looked over at Mother and gently said goodnight.

With my head resting on the pillow and my mind reflecting and absorbing the events of the night, I felt myself slipping over the edge. Could the phenomenon have some relation to the dark world of Navajo mythology? Could the eerie sounds have a connection to previous sins of the former occupants? In the past, I had occasions where my intuitive senses warned of impending danger. Was my intuition trying to accurately guide me with some kind of forewarning? I strained to hear the message. Nothing came but stony silence. My thoughts fragmenting and fading out of consciousness, I slept.

CHAPTER II

Awakening to a thin morning fog that seemed to radiate an eerie orange hue, I stared at the iridescent light filtering in through the curtains. Feeling a little foolish about my reaction the night before, I scrambled out of bed. What a glorious feeling to escape the suffocating heat of the Valley, I thought cheerfully. I opened the window and inhaled the crisp air. Temperatures back in Phoenix were predicted to reach a staggering one hundred sixteen degrees today.

Hearing a low rumbling sound and the honking of a horn, I quickly slipped into my jeans. "Mother, hurry along," I yelled, making a dash for the door. "I believe your prodigal son is here."

She was right behind me as we saw him walk in, smiling sheepishly. I studied the finely chiseled cheekbones that accentuated his expressive features. A rather tentative apologetic smile crossed his face as he continued along in his free-spirited gait. He wore his usual attire: blue faded Levi's, a short-sleeved shirt, and a pair of immaculate white tennis shoes. Perched incongruously on his head, fringed by tufts of his pale blonde hair, was one of his many caps bearing logos of his various businesses.

"It's amazing how predictable his facial expressions are," I muttered quietly. "Equally predictable is his lack of punctuality!"

Clayton never liked to be pinned down to specific obligations at specific times. His eyes rested on me, not knowing what kind of reception he would receive. I stood with my hands on my hips.

"Am I forgiven?" he asked, then without waiting for an answer, "Well, I see you two made it through the night. Did you hold a nocturnal vigil for the *Chindi*?"

Clayton's twinkling brown eyes melted away all feelings of indignation. He threw his arms around Mother and me. I was suddenly aware of the strong family love that bound us together. But his mention of the *Chindi* had somewhat dampened my cheerfulness. Inside the trading post, Clayton gestured expansively with the air of a proud proprietor. "Well, what do you think of my new enterprise?"

"To tell you the truth, Clayton, since we were confined to the bedroom most of the night, we haven't had much of a chance to explore," I responded.

"Well, five dollars will get you a tour, Sarah. Come on. Both of you."

The thick-beamed ceiling and mosaic rock floor of Clayton's game room, devoid of any furniture except for a pool table, identified it as part of the original structure. Centered in a now empty living room stood a simple fireplace with a plain wooden mantel. The trading post, mellowed with age, was eerily quiet even in the daylight hours. The appendages of the trading post stretched in different directions, forming cavities. As we explored the recesses of two more vacant rooms, purposefully designed as a dining room and kitchen, my footsteps were soft so as not to awaken the stillness or its memories. Not finding anything out of the ordinary, we continued to ramble throughout the old compound. What hidden secrets lay buried in its bowels? I could only wonder.

"What's this pole doing in my bedroom?" Clayton looked puzzled as he stood at the open doorway.

"That's my rod! I used it to ward off your '*Chindi*!'" I snapped.

Mother said, "Clayton, I don't know what she's talking about. I went to sleep."

"Don't be ridiculous, Sarah!" He looked at me, unable to suppress a patronizing smile.

I ignored him.

Moving past the bedrooms, we continued our way through the complex, its interior an intricate network—a warren of disjointed rooms. Separating the main house from the General Store was Clayton's office, one of the few rooms in this spacious citadel that showed any signs of occupancy. A faint light filtered from the adjoining room into this repository for his collection of papers, books, and other oddments. Commanding a large portion of space in this small niche was a huge walk-in safe. Its combination lock protected the treasures hidden behind the massive door. I felt certain that this particular area of the trading post was where invisible spirits dwelt. On the surface, the trading post and its living quarters appeared normal. Was its weathered old face camouflaging a lie? I couldn't seem to shake the lingering feeling of spookiness.

A unique aura surrounded this old fortress. My sixth sense picked up on a mysterious presence. I felt a fluttering inside me like a trapped bird. An electric tickle ran up my arms.

"Let's move on!" I heard my brother, his voice seeming to come from a distance.

"That suits me fine. This area of the trading post gives me the willies."

"You certainly have an active imagination!" Clayton rolled his eyes.

"You're right!" I paused and smiled. "You wouldn't have noticed that an evil was lurking unless it belched loudly and spewed green vomit all over the house!"

"Where do you get all these wacky ideas?" Clayton looked over at me.

"You know who else thinks the same way you do?" he said, wagging his finger at me. "People in the nut house, that's who. And they're not even playing with all their marbles!"

We returned to the small cozy kitchen equipped with the customary functional appliances. A glass case displaying an array of luscious homegrown fruits and vegetables divided the kitchen corner from the rest of the store. Beside the display case, I saw Camille. She was an attractive, pleasant-looking Navajo woman with beautiful dark eyes, who had arrived unnoticed to work. Clayton introduced us. Her thick black hair was drawn severely back from her face, exposing her sepia-colored skin and the traditionally high cheekbones passed down through the generations.

"I'll make some coffee," she said in a staccato-studded voice thick with accent. I watched her as she moved with a sense of almost ritualistic beauty and grace.

The hurried walk through the trading post had piqued my curiosity. I decided to explore the General Store and examine the wide variety of commodities stocked on its shelves. Coffee, flour, soft drinks, tobacco, and canned goods lined the well-stocked shelves. Everywhere I looked there were more shelves. Some were laden with hardware fixtures and plumbing supplies—everything from socket wrenches to tubes of epoxy glue. Cornmeal grinders and enameled coffeepots were displayed above Pendleton shirts and colorful shawls and blankets. Mounted on a narrow section of wall next to the shirts hung four custom leather saddles. Distinguished with its time-worn simplicity and useful functionality, the Blue Sage Trading Post & General Store remained much the same as it began: a local store servicing the several hundred souls spread out across this isolated land.

Coffee, permeating the air, enticed me with its aroma and beckoned me to the kitchen, as did my brother's voice. "Breakfast is ready!"

As we sat at the plain wooden table, a tablecloth giving it dignity, Clayton watched Mother as she talked with Camille. His expression as he gazed at Mother was one of admiration and love. Although he never told her, I knew he was proud of her accomplishments, especially her deep artistic talent.

Sipping my coffee, I studied the woman who had given birth to us. Pale blue eyes twinkled with merriment above the tips of her pink cheeks. A good-looking woman with a small, thin frame, she appeared to have eluded the effects of time. She had a quality about her, a sunny outgoing friendliness that always made people feel welcome. A markedly pleasant expression sparkled from her animated eyes beneath the rose-tinted glasses she wore. My mother viewed Clayton and the world through those glasses and from the same perspective.

In anxious anticipation, hoping our opinions would be favorable, Clayton asked again. "Well, folks, what do you think of this century-old landmark?"

Mother expressed her approval, but noticed there wasn't an empty shelf in the store, hinting that there was an apparent lack of customers.

"I think, Clayton...." I paused dramatically, knowing full well that I had his attention. Teasingly, I let him dangle in suspense. "One of the most attractive aspects of this place is that you are certain not to bump into anyone fashionable here."

He shook his head wryly. "That's just like you to make that remark," he said with exasperated fondness. "I'm surprised, Sarah, that you didn't wear your outdated mink coat, lizard cowboy boots, and flashy assortment of turquoise jewelry. Sarah's idea of dressing down for the occasion." He laughed at his own comment.

Apparently, Clayton's idea of breakfast was packaged pastries, which came in two varieties, blueberry or strawberry. Placing a blueberry pastry in the microwave, I stared blankly out the window, hardly noticing the gradual encroachment of light filling the kitchen. The early fog was lifting. After finishing my pastry, I arose and poured the last of the coffee into our cups.

"I don't know about the rest of you, but I'm about ready to continue the tour." Just as I spoke, I heard a deep masculine voice across the room.

"Do you want some gas?" the voice said.

The question came from a mahogany-skinned man who was wearing a green headband and a Pendleton plaid shirt. He was staring at us with huge remote eyes. Gnarled eyebrows accentuated his face and narrow cheekbones highlighted his flaws. In a stooped posture, not entirely a reflection of his age, he ploddingly came forward. Grinning broadly, he simulated an ingratiating smile that somehow did not seem genuine.

"I'd like you to meet my mother and sister," Clayton said. "This is Lenny. He and Camille are cousins; but then again, you will find that everybody here seems to be related to everybody."

Having made the introductions, and while engaging in a few pleasantries, Lenny repeated the question, this time speaking directly to me, "Do you want gas?"

"Yes! By all means, please fill it up. I'm sure it's on empty. I was planning to get my gas at Feldman's…" Judging from the expression on his face, I could tell he must have thought I was crazy. Rather than try to explain, I let him walk away in his slow gait.

"Would you like to see the wool room now?" Clayton asked. His tone and the expression on his face suggested something odd and unfavorable.

"Hurry up, Mother," he encouraged. "Come with us."

As we ambled our way outside, Clayton told us about the wool room, expounding on its significance. "In the past, the Navajos would charge their merchandise from fall to spring, paying their debts with wool after the shearing was finished. The wool room was where it was weighed and bagged. Later on, as the Indians received government subsidies, the room was mainly used to butcher sheep. I'm sure you'll find it interesting. There's a lot of history here."

"This is going to be so much fun," I said. "In all my travels, I've never seen a real Old West trading post."

Outside, next to the windmill, left over from the trading post's earliest incarnation, was a quaint stone building. It was constructed of walled-up stones laid in mud mortar, then plastered over with mud and straw.

Five buff-colored buildings circled the property to the west. A mountain rose to the east—a high rock formation with soaring stone spires and a broad, natural platform below.

"With any luck, today, we may see some bald eagles that are nesting a few miles from the property line." Clayton gestured toward the mountain.

It didn't take long to spot a trio of those majestic birds catching their breakfast next to the ridge. Nearby, we glimpsed some bighorn sheep. Huddled at the base, as if hugging the mountain, was an old deteriorating brown barn in partial ruin from years of neglect. The contiguous corral was also in disrepair with its timber decaying. Looking at the surrounding desolate landscape, so picturesque and unadulterated, I was intrigued by its simplicity. As if shunning the contemporary world, this place of remote antiquity seemed undisturbed by progress.

Although the wool room had accessibility from both the main house and the General Store, Clayton led us, not to those familiar entrances, but to an outside entrance accessible from the backyard. The door, hanging crookedly on its hinge, was ajar. Stepping through the tangled vegetation, I approached it warily. I peered in at the long narrow table, barely visible in the dark, dim room.

I looked at the table positioned beside me. The same one, I presumed, that originally was used to bag and weigh the wool, its thick pinewood reflecting its stature. Above the table, traces of light filtered in through the chicken wire that covered the bare windows, exposing the mass of gnarled vines creeping through the openings.

"Jeez!" Clayton yelled suddenly.

Whirling around, I turned to see him by an open freezer. He held up a long white cloth, stained with frozen blood. Exchanging glances, not knowing what to think, we stood bewildered, momentarily at a loss for words.

"I sure hope this is from a slaughtered animal," Clayton ventured.

"…Or, someone was murdered," I said, thinking back to last night's eerie wails. "And, I'm not being facetious either, Clayton. Nothing about this creepy place would surprise me. Why would anyone put bloody rags in the freezer anyway?"

"I don't know," he said. "Maybe it's from some kind of ritual." Pretending nonchalance, he shrugged, dropped the rags back in the freezer, and walked away.

I looked over at Mother. Her face was white.

Clayton noticed also and said, "Come; let me show you the view from the top of the mountain." He walked casually toward the ridge, as if he were the master surveying his domain.

We reached the edge where the hillside dropped away. From this vantage-point on top of the mountain, the world became a different place. The escarpment, resplendent in all its pristine beauty, seemed to dominate all nature below. Looking out from the precipice, I could see forever. Overhead, scudding white clouds floated above the rising bluffs, as a lone hawk silently made an arc, tracing an invisible pattern in the pale blue sky. The overwhelming sights and sharper awareness of nature put civilization in perspective. One felt a sense of freedom…a sense of space.

Clayton leaned back against the implacable face of a randomly placed boulder. He watched me as a few steps in any direction led me to magnificent panoramic views. Flashing a smile, he gloried in my approval.

"You'd better be careful, Sarah. It's a thousand-foot drop down," he cautioned. Turning toward Mother he stated, "Sarah always had a daring quality. It sounds ridiculous, but she seems to enjoy living her life on the edge." He laughed. "Nothing was ever uneventful," my little brother continued. "Sarah was always doing something exciting. There was the time that she and the boys 'had' to take a two-month safari in South Africa. If you remember, Mother," he paused, "first thing, Conner ended up falling. Naturally, there were no medical facilities within one hundred miles. And to top that, it was Sunday. However, Conner pulled through that one after Sarah finally rounded up some doctor in Johannesburg who was willing to perform the required surgery in his office. As if that wasn't enough excitement, they continued their journey flying with an African bush pilot in a private chartered plane and landed on a short dirt runway in the middle of the jungle. They stayed there one week in the thatched-roof roundovels at Mala Mala, an exclusive jet-setting game reserve in the Eastern Transvaal. To prevent intrusion from wild animals, a twenty-foot high bamboo fence had been constructed in front of a deep gully. You'd think Sarah would know that the 'moat' surrounding the property was not designed for the kids to play in. Another time, Sarah, at her sons' insistence, just 'had' to run the whitewater rapids of the Colorado River… But, I refuse to get into that story. It's too pathetic."

"Those were the good old days," I commented. "I don't feel very adventurous now!"

With the morning fog lifted, the diffused light from the sun's rays set the dunes ablaze in a white gold that radiated in all directions. After being in that damp, gloomy wool room, I still felt a chill. Outside, the sun felt rejuvenating as my skin absorbed its penetrating heat. We walked in the warmth of the day. Although sometimes the footing was soft, we navigated with ease for a couple of hours as we leisurely made our way back to have lunch. Upon our return to the house, Clayton went in and brought out box lunches that Camille had prepared, along with a pitcher of iced tea. Wild, green grass covered a patch of ground by the front door entrance next to the rutted yard. Breathing the cool, sweet air of the higher elevation, we all sat gathered together, exchanging accumulated news, sipping our tea, and eating our lunch.

Clayton, in his evasive manner, had an obstinate way of not letting me know what he was up to. I had to pry it out of him. During the intervals interspersed with questions, Clayton and I bantered back and forth, usually about nothing in particular. In one of her rare critical moments, Mother chastised him for leaving us alone the previous night and for frightening me. Hearing her express her disapproval and chide him for his faults, I was delighted with her reprimand. Nodding my head in agreement, I was unable to resist a grin.

"There must be a lot of stories about the trading post," I commented, taking a bite of apple, with my box lunch balanced on my knees. "Tell us about the background that formed its character, Clayton, and tell us some Indian legends too."

Clayton cleared his throat. "I'll be glad to give you some history about the trading post," he said with his shy yet cocky expression. "It was like this…"

"They had an established way of doing things here on the reservation back in 1903 when the trading post was built. It was founded on a bartering system. Wool, corn, beans and squash raised by the Navajo were exchanged for canned goods, clothing, and other staples. The Indian Trader, which is my official designation," he beamed, "allowed the Indians to charge their merchandise. In the spring, they would pay their debts with wool, and in the fall lambs were brought to the trader, who would keep them until they were sold to buyers or taken to the nearest shipping point.

"Now class, please feel free to raise your hands anytime you have questions," he said. Tipping back his chair in a precarious position, he continued.

"In those days, it was a ninety-mile commute by horseback to the nearest civilization, so the people who worked at the trading post also lived here, occupying those buildings that ring the property to the west," he said, nodding his head in that direction.

"Sheep have been part of the Navajo life since the 1600s. They are individually owned by the women in the family, but cared for in common. Tracing their descent through the maternal line, theirs is a matrilineal society, having something to do with their belief that the Earth is their Mother.

"Boys, in their society, attend the family sheep the way their fathers and grandfathers did," he continued. "The girls are taught to cook, process wool, and hand-weave the rugs that modern collectors prize so much.

"Speaking of that, Sarah, remind me after lunch to take you inside and show you where the store's finest rugs, pots, baskets, silver and turquoise, and even a few Kachinas are locked away.

"Although it looks much the same as it did back in 1903, there have been some noticeable changes in the post today. Wagon-wheel ruts and hoof prints have been replaced by tire tracks created by dusty pickup trucks.

No longer does water have to be hauled up the long, steep hill from the spring below, and electricity is now produced by our own diesel generator," he said proudly.

"People talk about the end of trading, the system of barter and exchange, but here, you can actually see it happening."

Listening attentively, my gaze fixed on my brother as he spoke of how Indian life was geared to the quiet desperation of survival. "Even today," he said, "it is a daily struggle, a hard life, especially during the harsh winters.

"Hogan homes still continue to be part of the lifestyle of the Navajos," he told us. "However, it is a society in transition. Younger people are not following the old traditions. They are abandoning their ancestral customs, their native tongue, and their native religion."

Hearing his words made me wonder…Will they fail to hold onto their center of harmony, their own peace? I guess nobody knows. For now, it is still a tribe that maintains its rituals of worship, chants and sings to heal their sick, tends its livestock, and curries the favor of its capricious gods, the *yeiibichai*.

"That's enough education for the day," Clayton declared, interrupting my thoughts. "There may be a pop-quiz later on!" he added.

I leaned back in my chair, a faint smile still across my lips as I contemplated all I had been told. Absorbed in thought, I looked into Clayton's smiling eyes. Was it my imagination or was there a hidden sadness? Was he affected by this lonely isolation? Was the solitude too empty? If there was sadness, it was kept secret, concealed beneath the veil of his eyelids. Clayton had begun a description of ancient Navajo lore, but his voice trailed off…

Behind us, the store was visible, and apparently his eye caught Camille, who was leaving for the day. Raising his arm in a sweeping gesture, he motioned her over. Her features registered surprise as I watched her come toward us.

"Camille, will you tell my mother and sister about the *Diné?*" he pleaded.

With a timorous demeanor, she hesitated. Then in a tentative voice, monosyllables somewhat disjointed, she eventually began to speak, in almost mystical cadences.

My People say,
Holy People put us here and this is our place.
A Sacred Land that the Holy People entrusted to our care.
The land given to us between the four mountains and four rivers was
to be our Dinetáh. The Holy People meant us to be in balance and
harmony with the Dinetáh—which is one and the same.
The Dinetáh is not only the Holy Land of the people, but also a way of life.

As Camille spoke, I captured the vision in my mind's eye. Sentinels that majestically reigned in quiet grandeur over the Dinetáh and its people…a people whose spirituality was derived from their souls.

I listened intently as she spoke of the Navajo origins in this beautiful and sacred land that was deeded to them by the gods of their forefathers. According to the legend, the Holy People created the World and formed the Earth into a livable place. These Holy People, she informed us, are believed to be the most powerful and significant deities in Navajo mythology. Like our Old Testament, the Navajo story contains a flood and expulsion from one world to another. The People passed through four lower worlds to emerge into this present Fifth World. The Story of Life begins in the First World, where it was predestined that living creatures, as well as inanimate elements, would come into being. The People inhabiting this dark First World, though spoken of as people, were insects, as we know them. Spiraling through passageways made by the wind, they emerged from these lower worlds.

Camille's voice had an exciting quality and lent itself to the dramatic narrative as she continued to talk about the Second and Third worlds. I found myself mesmerized by her lyric grace. Occasionally, she would close her eyes in meditation. I strained to listen.

The People inhabiting the Fourth World heard a voice calling. Three times more they heard the voice, each time nearer than before. Four mysterious beings appeared. Three times, these gods visited the People, but still did not talk. On the morning of the fourth day, the call of the gods was heard.

Speaking to the People in their own language, one of the gods told how they wished to make more people, but they wanted the forms of these people to be like themselves, not having the claw of the insect.

As instructed, the People placed two ears of corn, each with their tips pointed to the East, on a buckskin laid on the ground. Under the white ear, the gods put a feather from the white eagle, and under the yellow ear, a feather from the yellow eagle, and then they covered them with an upper buckskin.

The gods told the People to stand back to allow the Winds to enter. The White Wind blew from the East and the Yellow Wind from the West, blowing between the buckskins.

First Man and First Woman lay where the ears of corn had been: The white ear had been changed into a spirit man and the yellow ear into a spirit woman, the Winds giving them life.

That was how the two supernatural beings were created, she told us.

I sat quietly listening to the sweet melodious tone of her voice, gripped by the story. The sun sparkled off her large, medallion necklace as she lifted her face to the sky.

One day, the People were surprised to see a strange white light rise in the East. They sent the Locusts to see what it was. They returned to report that a vast flood was approaching from the East.

Soon the People were called to enter a reed, which was growing rapidly, spreading out, going up towards the surface of the earth. The reed grew higher and higher as they climbed. When they were all inside, the opening closed behind them, just as they heard the rush of the roaring flood waters.

According to the legend, it was from the Fourth World that the People, led by First Man and First Woman, emerged from the Underworld. A hole in the La Plata Mountains of southwestern Colorado is considered the place of emergence, Xajiinai.

The Diné believe that these major gods, the Holy People, created the present world using the earth brought from below. Not only the land itself, but also all forms of water, animals, and vegetation originated in the Underworld and were brought to the surface by the supernatural beings.

Listening intently as Camille moved through time in her journey from the womb of the world, I filed everything she said in my memory.

"Please, don't stop now," Clayton commented, as he glided past us on his way into the house to replenish the pitcher of iced tea. When he returned, Camille continued.

Ever-Changing Woman (representing the Earth or nature) first appeared magically as a baby girl clothed in light. Placed in a tiny cradle made of rainbows and laced back and forth with sunbeams through loops made of lightning, she was what the Holy People were wishing for. Ever-Changing Woman, wrapped in her cloak of many colored lights, later married Sun and Water. When a ray of light from the Sun, passing through drops of water from a waterfall, impregnated Changing Woman, she gave birth to her sons, the Twin War Gods.

This moment of creation is re-enacted today by shamans, the keepers of knowledge. The Blessingway Ceremony, the ceremony most sacred to the Navajo people, has come from this story.

Camille went on to describe how evil also existed in the form of monsters that came to infest the world. The Twin War Gods, according to the myth, succeeded in slaying many of the monsters that emerged from the Underworld. They failed, however, in disposing of old age, poverty, sickness and death. According to Navajo belief, their concept of an Afterworld is neither one of eternal punishment nor one of eternal bliss. The "land of the dead" is an ill-defined place, which is reached by four day's travel in a northerly direction after death. This next world is a world of the spirit, beyond which is a world where everything merges into the infinite universe.

She paused for a moment and took a sip of her iced tea. *They also believe death is inevitable and not to be feared as much as the dead themselves. Since the deceased are always a possible source of Chindi or malevolent spirits, they are ceremoniously disposed of as quickly as possible. Strict adherence to all performed rituals is required because an error might offend the deceased and cause the Chindi to seek revenge.*

"Where have I heard that before?" I wondered, glancing at Clayton, who gave me one of those, "I told you so," looks.

I clung to Camille's words when she spoke of intertwining details of Navajo tribal stories and myths. My thoughts were immersed in ancient beliefs and distant beginnings. I recalled the irresistible fascination I had felt when first being introduced to their culture, their art, and their spiritual beliefs. Had I ever lived among these people? A vision stirred dimly as of a memory: a long time ago…in her ancestral land, a girl covered in soft fringed leather…extends her arm, pointing to a horse. Standing in tall yellow grasses is a shadowy figure beside her…Was I experiencing a personal journey of discovery or was I fantasizing what I wished? For so long, I had been in an ambivalent spiritual malaise with a vague sense that there was something missing in my life. Today, exploring their culture more fully, I felt an even closer bond to the Navajo heritage…as if I was searching for a link that would draw me closer to my past.

I sensed that just as the shamans with their magical powers see with a vision normally not available to mortals, this trading post has a metaphorical life of its own, capable of exciting ordinary man to heightened revelations, a sphere of transformation and spirituality that is not his native realm. Although I suspected that the trading post was cursed, it was comforting to know that not even man's evil deeds could extinguish the "white light."

Interrupting my deep meditation, Clayton turned to me impetuously. "Come on, Sarah, I'm starving." He sprang out of his lawn chair. "I'm ready for dinner! Would you care to join us?" He looked over at Camille.

"No, thank you," she said, as she got up to leave. "I have to go now."

"What's on the dinner menu for tonight, Clayton? Do we have any choices?" I asked, as we made our way into the house, then to the kitchen. He took a frozen packet from the freezer. "No! Please, Clayton. Not liver and onions," I said, turning up my nose at his first suggestion. "How could you even consider that, especially after seeing those bloody rags in the freezer?"

"Trust me. It won't be that bad. I'll try not to serve it blood rare," he grinned. "Here, Sarah, you can wash it down with this." He handed me a bottle of Cabernet Sauvignon wine.

"Thank you, Clayton. That is sweet of you. It's my favorite and Mother's favorite, too, although you shouldn't have gone to the bother…"

"Shut up! Sarah," he said, playfully.

"Clayton?" I kind of hesitated.

"What is it, Sarah?"

"Do we have to have liver and onions?"

"I'm so sorry, Madame. I regret that you find my choice unacceptable, but we seem to be out of the sauce for the Duck à L'Orange," he smirked. "What do you think this is, a gourmet restaurant?"

Mother looked at Clayton and said, "Please, Clayton, don't you have something else besides liver and onions? I agree with Sarah."

"Let me see what I can come up with." Clayton put the liver back in the refrigerator and took out a package of chicken breasts, along with a bag of yellow potatoes. "Sarah, you could offer to help."

He removed three potatoes and started applying the peeler. "It frightens me to see you so isolated up here," I said ruefully, as Mother and I continued to sip our wine.

"I'm sorry about that bit that happened in the wool room. I know that sometimes some really weird stuff goes on around here."

"Clayton, I'm not psychic, but I can tell you, you can core all the way down to what I guess you'd call the id…although it's awful down there, full of the most monstrous images…like those scorpion fish they find in the ocean, the ones with the venomous spines on their dorsal fin. And you still wouldn't find anything as evil as what's in this house."

For a second there was no sound but the birds singing outside.

"Anyway, all I get from you is surface stuff, and most of *that* is skewed and distorted. If you were like anyone else, I'd know what's going on with you, and why you look so worried…"

"Thanks, Sarah, I knew there was a reason I invited you here. Since it's not the esprit de corps, it must be the intrusiveness. He grinned, but it was a nervous grin. He peeled another potato.

"As it is," Clayton went on, as if I hadn't criticized him, "I can make some educated guesses as to what went on in the wool room, but that would only feed your overactive imagination."

"All right," I said, although it wasn't all right…nothing was right. "Who or what are they besides the *Chindi*? Are they demons? Skinwalkers? Poltergeists?"

"I invited you up here because I wanted you to get some relaxation and rest," Clayton said. "I didn't expect that you would encounter the *Chindi*!"

"I realize that. Neither did I." A smile ghosted around the corners of my mouth. "A few more encounters and I'll be ready for a straightjacket."

"Your problem, Sarah, is that you see too much. Half of the time, I don't know if your fantasies are real or imagined."

"That's not very fair, Clayton," I snapped. "Take art, for example. It hardly does a painting justice to just glance at it. If you keep looking at it, the doors of perception open, entering upon the mystical level…I experienced that today, Clayton."

"You had better not let anyone else, other than family, hear you talk like that," he interrupted. "Or you're liable to be labeled 'certifiably insane.' Do you think you experienced some sort of enlightenment today?" he said, grinning. "Whether it's a mystical revelation or merely hallucination hardly matters. If you want my opinion, it sounds like a delusional psychotic.

"Speaking about spirituality," he continued, "the Navajo have a superstition that certain objects have a powerfully beneficial influence. A talisman, manifesting magical powers, saves you from evil by warding off demonic spirits." His voice wavered in a spooky undertone. "It just so happens, I have one right here," he continued smugly, slapping his pant's pocket. "The other day when I was out in the yard, I found this stone with some sort of design etched on its surface," he said, while fishing in his pocket. "It certainly doesn't have much artistic merit, but it might be a talisman.

"Incidentally, Sarah, in case you didn't know, there are ancient burial sites scattered throughout this entire property. In fact, the trading post is practically built on one. With that tidbit of information, I can almost guarantee she'll be up all night," he chuckled to Mother. "Listening for the *Chindi*," he droned.

"Stop teasing your sister!" Mother said, as I reached over as if to slap him. I curiously looked at the flat, dull stone as he placed it in my hand. It felt warm to the touch.

"You can have it, Sarah. Judging from the experiences you go through, you'll probably need it more than I."

"I hope this stone is a harbinger of good fortune," I thought aloud, "and not a charm that's bewitched," I murmured under my breath, as if the spirits might be listening.

Although undistinguished, the grilled chicken and mashed potatoes that Clayton prepared for us were strengthening. Feeling satisfied, we resumed our respective positions in the front yard. The suggestion of chill was in the air. I sat curled up in my chair. I inhaled deeply, as if breathing in new life.

"I can see why you chose this lifestyle," I sighed.

My mind, pleasantly adrift in a sea of thought, receded back in time to when Clayton, upon receiving his degree in business, had announced his plans to enter law school. Naturally, he chose a school in California, renowned for its students' tans. Our father, I recalled, was ecstatic with Clayton's decision to further his education and never failed to give him encouragement and advice. Dad, by a long systematic process of engaging in advance study, had acquired an enormous amount of knowledge in various fields. He had a Master's degree in music, was a college professor, and a distinguished concert violinist. He also was a metallurgist, a scientist, and a professor of science, who even taught his course in Russian. Dad was a true scholar. Obviously, he had profound respect for education, but commonplace ordinary occurrences simply aroused no interest. My brother eventually followed in his footsteps as far as education, whereas my ambition was to travel. My father's untimely death from congestive heart failure left bittersweet memories. Whenever I listened to a concert, I always thought of him.

Stretching back in his chair, Clayton brought me back, continuing where Camille, earlier in the day, had left off. I listened eagerly as he explained that for the early Navajos, as in other parts of the world today, priest and physician were one. According to Indian beliefs, health is a state of balance and harmony, something holy. They also believe that the condition of the spirit determines the physical state of the body; that sickness is a disruptive imbalance and is usually the manifestation of malevolent forces.

"Clayton!" I said intently with my eyes fastened on his. "Do you know anything about Navajo ceremonies, of the medicine men with their curative powers and their special chants?"

"I'm getting to that, Sarah. I've been told that there are probably over fifty chants or 'ways' and that's not counting the variations. Can you believe it takes from five to ten years just to learn one ceremony?

"Through these ceremonial rituals, the Holy Ones, the *yei,* can be encouraged to assist with supernatural powers. It is customary to use chants, prayers, dances, prayer sticks, plants, sweat lodges, sand paintings…The list goes on.

"Illness is caused by disharmony, and every effort is made to overcome it through the correct use of ceremonial objects and substances, restoring the patient to perfect harmony. But first, the 'hand trembler' has to diagnose the illness. Using prayer and some sacred pollen causes the medicine man's hands to tremble when applied to the patient, thus determining the exact illness.

"On one occasion, I was allowed to witness a hand trembling ceremony," Clayton said. "During the ritual, I remember watching the shadow of a trembling hand and arm in front of me and listening to the incantations. I used to think it was all 'smoke and mirrors,' but not any more.

"Once the patient is diagnosed and the proper ceremony is determined to produce the required healing, it's my understanding that the patient then goes through the lengthy, complicated and expensive curing rites. Obtaining power from the specific deities whose help is sought, he is able to overcome the evil causing the sickness. Once again, after he has been restored to harmony, he 'Walks in Beauty'."

"Oh, Clayton! I would I love to watch one someday!" I said excitedly.

"Well, Sarah, if you ever have an occasion to witness such an event, just remember they also conduct what's called the 'Enemy Way.' Originally a war ceremonial, now it is performed for persons whose sickness resulted from contact with white people, *belagahnah*. How does that make you feel?" he asked with a grin.

"They have chants for just about everything. I'm told that The Windways, caused by evil winds, cures a host of illnesses from poor vision to tuberculosis to even heart trouble."

"Clayton, how do you suppose the body reveals the area affected, allowing the healer to feel the sensation? I know our doctors use some sort of heat-sensitive instrument, in a procedure called thermography, which registers differences in body heat caused by injury, illness or disease. Could evidence of that heat be felt by the hand trembler?"

"That's a thought, Sarah, although the hand trembler has to possess a certain gift. Navajos believe that the gift of seeing what is inside a person comes from the Gila monster. Not everyone can be a hand trembler. He must possess the spirit of the large venomous lizard. Although hand tremblors, stargazers, and crystal gazers don't like to be compared to psychics, astrologers, or fortune tellers, in many ways they play the same roles," he concluded.

"Once, when I was young, I went to a psychic who read tea leaves," I said. "She predicted that I would travel all over the world. I couldn't imagine that I would ever be so lucky. She also said I would marry and have two wonderful sons. So far, my destiny has been fulfilled, just as she promised."

"There may be something to it. Who knows?" Clayton turned towards Mother.

"Back to what we were talking about," he said, "the sand painting may require a dozen or more people, working most of the day, to complete. From what I understand, the Navajos, using natural pigments and dyes, have mastered almost a thousand separate, symbolic designs. During the large ceremonials, sand paintings are executed within a hogan, often specially built for the ritual. The patient is brought in and seated upon the dry painting. The medicine man then takes sand from certain symbolic sections of the design and rubs it onto the patient. Upon gaining power from the gods, the sand absorbs the evil that has caused the sickness. And, wait until you hear this," he chortled, "the intricate painting is then ceremoniously buried. Can you imagine all that creative art being destroyed—in the same day it is produced?

"There are four Sacred Plants that one sees in many sand paintings: corn—which is their most important crop—squash, beans and, you can appreciate the last one, Sarah, tobacco." Clayton didn't smoke, but he never missed an opportunity to chide me for my bad habit.

"Occasionally, peyote is used where color visions are actually experienced and can even be 'heard' speaking," he said. "The effects wear off, I'm told, within twenty-four hours, and it is non-habit forming, leaving no ill after effects."

"Are you suggesting, Clayton, that perhaps I should smoke peyote instead of cigarettes?"

"No, what I'm implying is that it appears you already have been!"

"Very cute!" I muttered. "I suppose you're referring to last night?"

"Now, why would you think that?" He sighed, rolling his eyes. "Do you think I could be alluding to your recent dismal lapse of mind?" he asked, snickering. "You had better take up writing fiction. You've certainly got the imagination for it."

The sun was setting low, nearly blocked from view, as if behind a thick gauze curtain. Lightning flashed across the horizon. The clouds moved in, their slate-covered haze covering the sky, turning the peaks a blue gray. I wanted Clayton to continue, but it was getting late. Lumbering thunderheads rolled voluminously overhead as the lightning illuminated the darkness. The old juniper tree still loomed grotesquely.

It was from that same corner of the house that the eerie "sounds" emanated last night. I caught myself looking for macabre forms hidden behind the trees. "Perhaps, we had better call it a day," I suggested. "It looks like…" Before I was able to finish my words, the storm broke. The first thunder crashed as the black clouds ruptured, and the lightning forked a jagged electric blue through the clouds. We ran for the shelter of the house. When we got to the entrance, I looked up. The flash from the stark blue sepulchral light filtered down, as if inspiring a memory of those entombed below me. Remembering what Clayton had told me about this place being built on a burial ground, I wondered what else was buried beneath the floorboards or lurking in the rafters.

It was nearly midnight before the house was completely still. Clayton had tried twice before to get us to retire, reminding us how Camille encouraged "getting up early to greet the sun." But we were all having such a good time. Only after Clayton had made an obvious gesture of looking at his watch and yawning, did we clear the glasses from the table and turn out the lights. Mother and I retired to Clayton's bedroom, and he climbed into his sleeping bag in the hallway.

After the rain, the skies cleared, leaving the way open for the light of the moon. From the window, I could see the tips of the grass glistening. In the light, it resembled a moonglade, the lighted path the moon makes over the water as it shimmers. "Just being here is so refreshing," I whispered thankfully, as I reached over and turned down the blinds.

Standing in front of the walnut dresser, I stepped back, regarding my visibly relaxed face in the beveled-glass mirror. "I hope tonight's proceedings don't take another lurch into the surreal," I said aloud. I was not anticipating anything unfavorable, but was not ruling out nightmarish possibilities. I looked over and saw that Mother was fast asleep. Rethinking and savoring the day's tales, I picked up the small, carved stone. In the glow of the light, its dull surface sparkled with tiny flecks of turquoise color, giving it a burnished effect. I held it in my hand. Breathing faintly and closing my eyes…letting the realm of mythology guide me and the invisible forces aid me, I prayed, asking the spirits' blessings, and willing away the ghosts.

I slept soundly. Nothing disturbed my sleep.

When morning dawned, I was refreshed. Clayton greeted me in the hall on my way to the kitchen. "What time is it?" he groaned, rubbing his eyes as he crawled out of his sleeping bag.

"Six o'clock!" I chimed cheerfully.

Clayton meandered over to the map spread across the kitchen table, as Mother entered the room, smiling.

"Is there anything in particular you two would like to see today?"

Mother, with her malleable personality, was agreeable to any suggestions. So he sat, waiting for my response.

"I was hoping that we could go over to Hubbell's Trading Post," I said.

"Of course! I should have guessed. Leave it to you to find a tourist trap. And I suppose you'd like to buy some authentic Indian artifacts, too."

"Maybe," I answered, knowing that was precisely what I intended to do.

"Don't you think you got in enough trouble with all the antiques you bought that time in Europe? Or have you forgotten?"

"No! I haven't forgotten how I was detained by every custom's official in every country because I didn't have the required letters of authenticity."

"And, what else, Sarah?"

"Okay, you made your point Clayton. I won't try to purchase any ancient Indian relics."

"Not only that, Sarah, Hubbell's happens to be in the opposite direction. I was planning to take a drive toward Hopi Land, an area west of here, completely surrounded by the Navajo Reservation. On the way, I thought you might enjoy the spectacular drive through Keams Canyon, that being just one of the various points of interest."

"Clayton, don't you think we'd be able to fit in Hubbell's today?" I persisted.

"Oh, all right, Sarah!" he acquiesced. "Now, is there any place else?" he breathed with exasperation.

My resistance paid off. Just south of the Ganado turnoff sprawled the stately Hubbell Trading Post. The rambling old hacienda was like a living museum, displaying its ancient relics and crafts. Rugs of varied traditional tribal patterns covered the floors and walls. There were stacks of newly hand-woven rugs, all having the authentic smell of hand-spun wool, each in a different size with remarkable colors. Leisurely, I inspected the famous regional Ganado Red weaving style, observing the red diamonds woven on a gray background and also observing the price. The white tag, fastened carefully to its corner, marked $9,000, did not seem like a great bargain to me, but what did I know?

Made by well-known artisans, the distinctive Navajo silver set with chunks of turquoise had a fine art quality, similar to that which you might find in the galleries along the exclusive Canyon Drive in Santa Fe; again, with a price tag to match.

Hanging on the wall above me, was a painting of Ever-Changing Woman. I couldn't take my eyes from it. Changing Woman, "in one hand holding an ear of corn and in the other a corn tassel containing pollen," is the most preeminent of the supernatural beings, for she symbolizes fertility and regeneration and the bringing of all green things to life year after year. It was Changing Woman… "a rainbow necklace around her neck made from the sacred stones from the four sacred mountains—white shell, turquoise, coral, and jet—who created human beings using flakes of skin from her own body."

Displayed behind the counter was an ancient *yeibichai* mask. It reminded me of something that Camille had told us. Yeis, the male and female figures that represent such forces of nature as wind, thunder, and lightning were included with the lesser deities. I tried to recall her exact words as she related how the Navajo personify the elements.

Sifting through the words that formed in my mind, it was coming back, but I was unable to get it exactly right. "The 'He' rain is the violent thunderstorm that drives the seeds into the earth; the 'She' rain is the gentle rain that nurtures the soil, bringing all green things to life. The 'rainbow' is considered to be the path of the *yei*. Because much damage can occur from the elements, these divinities are invoked by prayer and song so that no harm will come to the D*iné*."

My thoughts interrupted, I heard someone say, "Let's not spend all day here." I turned to see Clayton heading out the door.

Hubbell's, with its landmark status, in this small remnant community of the old west had been interesting and fun. Unlike the 'no frills' ambiance of the Blue Sage Trading Post & General Store, this legendary post catered to the whims of the tourist.

Although tempted to visit awhile longer, we continued our journey in a circuitous route past the Presbyterian Church and the Ganado mission. Looking at the Spanish Colonial architecture of the old mission, I couldn't help but think of the European clerics who came here decades ago. They were theologians, a body of religious scholars; ever anxious to conquer a "primitive" civilization, yet blind to its own savagery; ever anxious to enlighten a backward people, but always reluctant to learn from them.

Tracing along the border of a steep ravine, we threaded our way through a series of gouged out canyons showing the effects of a huge prehistoric flood. "In case you haven't already guessed, you are now viewing Keams Canyon," Clayton informed us. As the road meandered, hugging precipitous cliffs, he kept up a steady patter about the sights around us.

"Tell you what" he said suddenly, thinking fast, and veering the car onto another roadway. "There's a small, Mexican restaurant somewhere in this direction. We can stop and indulge in a little food and drink before we head for home. How does that sound to you?"

"Sounds great to me," I said. The nerve endings traveling to my brain registered pangs of hunger. "Is that okay with you, Mother?" I asked.

She amiably agreed.

The road wandered from stark lifeless arroyos to an almost pastoral setting.

A small flock of dingy white sheep crossed the road before us. A little boy followed the sheepherder, who was moving his flock up the trail to pasture on the Rim. A mongrel dog trailed behind him. We remained stopped just long enough to hear the tinkle of sheep bells and to watch them as they all disappeared into the landscape. A cow on a nearby hill bawled scoldingly as cattle roamed the grazing land in the valley below. The rural agrarian area—and little else—stretched northward. It felt as if we were in the middle of nowhere. No one was in sight.

"Where do the people live?" I wondered, as I remained preoccupied in thought.

As if reading my mind, Clayton commented, "It's remarkable how a hogan can be hidden from view. The isolated dwellings, sometimes as many as three or four in a group, are usually well concealed in the thick clusters of trees. Hogans can best be seen at night. Then, you can distinguish the smoke as it rises, curling upward from the smoke hole in the center. Not only can you see them clearly, scattered throughout the vast blackness, but you can detect their presence in the air tinged with the aromatic flavor of pinon."

Two hours later, in the late afternoon, we pulled into the gravel lot of the restaurant. I was surprised that our car was the only one there.

"Guess I was just plain lucky to get reservations," Clayton quipped, unable to resist the opportunity for such a remark.

Festive tablecloths adorned the tables in front of a colorful mural painted on the wall. We scanned the menu that offered mostly Mexican food.

"Sarah, I see nothing is wrong with your appetite," Clayton said, as he watched me eat in ravenous pleasure when the fiesta platter was set before me.

After dinner, driving back on Navajo Route 4, we finally approached the familiar stony ramparts of nearby Black Mountain. From the trading post one could see the huge, sloping, yellow-ochre monolith rising abruptly from the basin floor. I wondered why they named it "Black" Mountain.

The summer sun was setting low on the horizon as we arrived at the main yard of the trading post. Exhausted and having tucked away the thoughts and the sights of the day in my memory to rethink later in my room, Mother and I bid each other goodnight as she retired to the bedroom. After nightfall, I went outside to the quiet sounds of nature filling the darkness. Every star in the heavens sparkled as I looked up into the infinite space. The nighttime stars, created by Fire God, were like distant campfires, glowing like the dark mysteries of the universe. The sun was down and another day had passed. Time seemed to stand still. I looked for smoke and listened for the far off rhythm of drums.

As the early dawn broke and the sky brightened a shade lighter, I realized a happiness not recognized before in greeting the new rising sun. Given the enchantment of this place, it was with considerable regret that I finished packing my suitcase.

Although unable to join us, Clayton had arranged a guided Jeep tour for Mother and me of the legendary Canyon de Chelly, pronounced "deeshay," meaning "between the rocks." Throughout the one hundred thirty square mile canyon network were ancient cliff dwellings carved in red sandstone walls. I was excited to see the perpendicular cliff dwellings that had been the home of the Anasazi for over eight hundred years.

"Have a good time," Clayton waved. "Should you fancy an arrowhead lying on the ground, don't pick it up."

"Don't worry, I won't."

In Canyon de Chelly the beauty was bestowed upon visitors and natives alike. Many other curious tourists joined us in the six-wheel-drive truck that transported us down into the depths of the wide floor of the canyon. The perpendicular walls carved with petroglyphs and decorated with pictographs, rose seven hundred feet from the sandy bottom, where groves of peach trees thrived. Scattered among the cottonwoods at the bottom of the canyon were the octagonal hogans, where Navajos still lived and farmed.

Our guide told us how, "In ancient times, the Anasazi, predecessors of the modern Pueblo, lived in the dwellings ingeniously constructed within the high cliffs. Later, the canyons served as a Navajo stronghold." The Navajos appropriately named the canyon "Fortress Rock." The levels were connected by log poles, which were pulled up behind them. The Navajo survived for months while Kit Carson waited below. The army burned the houses and orchards in the canyon and killed the sheep. Eventually running out of food and water, the People came down from the caves.

Our guide also talked about the "Long Walk" in 1864 when 8,500 Navajos were forced to relocate to sparse land four hundred miles away. Many Navajos from Canyon de Chelly perished. Some survivors did not return from Fort Sumner, New Mexico, when they were released four years later. Only a "handful" of twenty-eight clans came back.

At the end of our excursion, Mother and I spent the night at a local motel, even though we had little more than a toothbrush and a change of clothes. After having had a good night's sleep, we were ready to embark on our journey back home. But first, we stopped at the trading post to say our farewells and to gather up our belongings. As I stood in the open doorway of the trading post, I felt myself shiver, as suddenly I became aware of an instinctive feeling. My eyes rested on Clayton. I was helpless to explain what I felt, frightened for reasons that I didn't fully understand.

"Clayton," I finally said, despondently, "I have such mixed feelings about this place. There's something very strange going on. I feel what happened the other night was about as strange as it gets. You had better observe some basic precautions," I added.

"Will you stop worrying needlessly?" he said with his hand closed tightly over mine. "I'll be fine here, Sarah," he said, as he squeezed gently.

"I'll say no more, Clayton. Just, please, be careful," I implored, knowing that he seldom heeded my advice.

Packing the last of our bags in the trunk, we stood by the side of the car. My eyes stretched outward for one final glimpse of the offered vistas. It was like looking beyond the ends of the earth. Hugging Clayton and giving him our blessings, Mother and I said goodbye. We began to motor down the dust-choked, earth-packed track. Looking back, I watched Clayton as he raised his arm, waving and smiling, until he disappeared from view. Undoubtedly, this road to the "mythical kingdom" would be among the most indelible images from this journey. Descending, winding our way down through the immense stone gateway, was like leaving an inner sanctum—a sanctuary for the soul.

The trip home to the Valley was long. While driving steadily, I reflected on how I loved old things: old walls, mission churches, old objects of art. To me they were an expression of continuity in life, giving it meaning. Although drained from the long and tedious drive, I returned home filled with the excitement of unknown places and adventure, enriched beyond measure and thrilled with a feeling that I had, "walked among the Ancients."

After a long day and many miles, we reached the edge of my driveway. Mother took her suitcase and put it in her car. I retreated inside to fix dinner. Home again. Back to the routine. I took out my crock pot, ready for spicy chili and home-baked bread. Too bad Mother couldn't have stayed for dinner.

I cooled my hands around a frothy glass of mango juice and sniffed appreciatively at the aroma of fresh bread wafting from the oven. After dinner, I was off to bed, already planning another "walk among the Ancients" with Clayton. But that would not happen.

CHAPTER III

Early one morning in mid-December, while finishing the remainder of my breakfast of eggs basted in butter, I picked up the morning newspaper. Perusing it, my eyes rested on an article titled, "Unsolved Mysteries." It featured the numerous murders committed, specifically in Arizona, which to-date remained unsolved.

Scanning the list, about half way down the page, my eyes widened in shock as I stared at the words: "1982: Teenage boy…brutally murdered… both he and his dog found shot to death…at the Blue Sage Trading Post on the Navajo Reservation." The article reported that the victim, who was killed by an intruder(s) while asleep on the sofa, was the owner's son. "… As yet, no suspect has been found."

The hairs rose on the back of my neck.

Immediately, I picked up the phone. Although still too stupefied to speak, I dialed Clayton's number.

The phone rang…and rang. But there was no answer. The only sound I heard was some static on the line as I waited in shocked silence. Just as I was about to hang up, Clayton finally answered.

"Why didn't you tell me there had been a murder up there?" I asked angrily, a wave of anxiety washing over me as I waited for him to answer.

"How did you find that out?" he questioned.

"It was in today's paper. That's how. I can't believe you didn't tell me."

"Well, I suppose I better tell you what I know," he said hesitantly. "You probably won't rest until I do," he sighed.

"John Morgan, the deputy sheriff, was the previous owner of the trading post before I took over the operation. About five years ago, Morgan's son was found killed, gunned down while asleep on the sofa, with a bullet they believe was intended for his father."

Incredulously, I listened, as he told me the whole story, including some of the speculative rumors circulating around the crime.

His voice rumbled into the phone as he explained, "The mystery of his death lay heavily upon the trading post. That's one of the reasons why the Indians believe this place is haunted with an evil force," he said in conclusion.

"Why didn't you tell me that when I was up there in August?" I demanded.

"If I had, Sarah, it probably would have pushed you over the edge," he said, beginning to ridicule my behavior that day.

"I knew it wasn't my imagination." In trying to ease my annoyance and allay my fears; his remark did little to reduce my sense of foreboding.

With my mind reeling, I attempted to convey my feelings, while trying to erase the memory of those eerie sounds screaming out of the dark.

"Well, Sarah, you're not the only one who has an uneasy feeling about this place," he confessed. "I thought I had found someone to manage the trading post for me. This lady, whom I've known for years, was so excited at the prospect of working up here that it seemed odd to me when she didn't show up."

"And why didn't she?" I prompted, marveling at the calmness of my voice.

"Later that day, when she called to offer her apology, she explained that she had intended to be here as scheduled, but half way from Phoenix, she turned around."

"Go on, Clayton!" I sensed he was avoiding having to tell me something as he reluctantly continued.

"Apparently, Sarah, she has psychic abilities, or so she says. She felt that if she worked at the trading post as planned, she would be killed." He stopped short. "I have to get going, Sarah," he said abruptly. "Some of us have to work, you know."

"Before you go, Clayton" I interjected quickly, not wanting to press the issue. "Can you plan to be here around midday on Christmas?"

"Noon on Christmas," he confirmed, and with a few perfunctory words of parting, we hung up.

I drooped in my chair. Sitting alone at the table, I felt a shiver run over my flesh. For the remainder of the day, emotions swept through me as I thought about the isolation and remoteness of Clayton's surroundings.

That night, in the darkness of my bedroom, many thoughts churned in my mind. What forces do we set in motion when we willfully wound one another? Was there a damaged soul out there seeking redemption? Or a vindictive spirit seeking revenge?

I didn't sleep well that night. I woke up often from terrible dreams and got up early the next morning, feeling uneasy and depressed. Even the sunshine did little to dispel my somber mood.

Christmas was only a few days off. Today was a bright sunny day. How I wished I could see the snow, I thought to myself, as I stared out the window, but not much chance of that in the Valley of the Sun. I supposed the forthcoming holiday was distracting me by stirring up memories as well as half-formed hopes.

I had combed the stores earlier in the day, bringing stacks of packages home with me. Preston, who would be celebrating his twenty-first birthday in January, and Conner, preparing for his nineteenth just three days after Christmas, were difficult to shop for, having acquired a specific "preppy taste."

With thoughts of Christmas still filling my mind, I dreamily recalled the time when we had spent the holidays at the family cabin. Pictures seemed to flash in my mind, springing to life of their own accord. Although almost ten years had passed, it seemed like only yesterday.

It was the day before Christmas…The great white flakes had begun falling early that morning. We had all clambered into Clayton's Jeep, setting out to find an off-the-highway roadway where we could choose and cut a tree. I remembered how the snow, swirling and spiraling on the front of the windshield, made it almost impossible to see. On a back road, deep with snow, we found the perfect spot.

We searched the forest, trekking over the land, which was blanketed in hummocks of snow. Conner was mainly interested in the size of the tree, wanting the biggest tree he could find in the middle of the piney woods.

Preston was more particular, studying each one from every angle and examining it for symmetry and structure. He must have been around ten years old at the time, but even in earlier years, I recalled, he had always searched for perfection. In doing so, he sometimes allowed himself to become a slave to an impossible set of standards.

Clayton had been leaning on the ax handle. Having found the ideal tree, he picked up the ax and began chopping. As I looked wistfully at the boys playing in the snow, Preston scooped up a handful of fresh snow and pelted Conner enthusiastically with the powdery balls, laughing when Conner's return shots slammed him in the face.

I remembered thinking that there was nothing like this back home in Phoenix. On the rare occasions when snow dusted the ground, it melted quickly, being no more than a phenomenon at which we all marveled.

"I'm waiting, Sarah," I recalled Clayton saying, as he stood in the doorway of the cabin. "Where do you want me to set up the tree? I can't hold it all day." He sighed impatiently, his lips pressed together tightly with a tolerant sort of exasperation on his face. But two hours later, when our laughing quartet had finished its work, even Clayton had to admit that his "tree" with silver tinsel dripping from every branch and white garlands of popcorn strung elaborately over its boughs had become a beautiful Christmas tree. The crowning touch was Gucci's red stocking cap on top of the tree, lapped over with bells dangling from the tip of the tassel, adding its own creative touch.

Drawing on the memories of that earlier Christmas and savoring the fragment of the past, I realized how fortunate I was. That joy was the source of our family's strength and had helped to shape us throughout our lives.

The next few days went by quickly as I busied myself with holiday tasks. Before I knew it…it was Christmas.

I woke early after a short night's sleep, anticipating the excitement of the day, just as the first gray light of dawn outlined the eastern horizon.

By noon, the marvelous aroma of the Christmas turkey had filled the whole house. Putting the finishing touches on the supremely elegant holiday table, I stood back, pleased with the effects of my work.

My mind drifted as I recalled how I had traveled half way around the globe in search of the beautiful pieces. Sometimes, I missed my young single days when I used to fly as a flight attendant for Northwest Airlines. As I sat admiring the French inlaid desk, unquestionably authentic to the trained eye, I longed for the celebration to begin. In anticipation, I placed a cassette in the recorder, the same one that I played every year on Christmas day. Hearing the sweet tinkling music-box sounds of my favorite Christmas songs, my spirits were soothed.

As I straightened an ornament on the tree, I became aware of the two charismatic young men sprightly walking across the room. My sons were home for the holidays.

"Good morning, Mother," they said in unison. "Merry Christmas!" Drawing me into the curve of their powerful arms, they bent to press their cheeks against mine, as I reached up to kiss each of them.

"Merry Christmas!" I said jubilantly with a sudden surge of exhilaration.

Preston and Conner resembled each other in so many ways, and the two years that separated them always seemed much less. Brilliant students, both had a confident facility with words and startlingly original and illumined minds. How fascinating they were to watch as they sparred in verbal matches, one trying to out do the other. Preston and Conner did irritate each other from time to time, especially when they were young, but rarely did they resort to blows. Perhaps, because in earlier years, both were required to sit on the "punishment chair," regardless of who was at fault. A little sibling rivalry is natural as long as it's not mean-spirited. Now they were incredibly handsome, gifted young men.

"Merry Christmas!" Another holiday greeting came from Clayton as he rushed in through the door. "I know, I'm late!" He tilted his face in greeting, waiting for me to kiss his cheek.

He knew he had been forgiven when I kissed it lightly. "Well, if it isn't the land baron of Cornflower Corners!" I teased, as I headed back to the kitchen. It was a term that I often used when referring to him, since he owned the largest block of property in that tiny town. "What was the problem Clayton? Couldn't you get across the 'crick'?" I jeered, recalling how he had mentioned that when the "crick was up" everyone on the other side would be stranded.

Ignoring my comments, Clayton casually drifted over to the oven. "What happened to the turkey?" he asked, flinging open the oven door and then slamming it shut. "Did you forget to defrost it?"

"Keep your wit to yourself," I bristled, jabbing at him with my finger.

"One thing I can say, Sarah, at least it has character," he admitted. "I hope you remembered to remove the giblet bag this time...before you stuffed the gobbler," he added, deliberately reminding me of a past culinary error.

"That was a long time ago, Clayton," I protested, glancing over at Preston, who was standing in the kitchen observing our banter. Preston's smile deepened, folding itself into dimples at the corner of his mouth.

"Hi, Uncle Clayton!" he said, unable to contain his deep joyous laugh.

"Merry Christmas, Preston," Clayton said cheerfully, handing him a gift-wrapped parcel "Where's your brother?" We heard a faint sound that became increasingly louder as Conner walked merrily into the room humming a Christmas carol.

Mother arrived. She gave big hugs to Clayton and my boys. "It's so good to see all of you."

After the boys exchanged greetings with Clayton and Mother, we all moved toward the living room. Looking proudly at my sons, I felt so warm and happy watching them together. God willing, they would live a long time and always have each other. A sibling's bond is forever. We were all noisy and cheerful as we settled closer to the tree to open our gifts. I watched happily as everyone exchanged packages with anticipation, ripping away the layers of paper.

Mother seemed delighted with the lavender-flowered cloth travel and garment bag designed especially for weekend excursions. "Thank you, Sarah," she said, reaching over to hug me warmly.

Clayton opened one of his packages to find a book tucked inside. He frowned when he read the title, *Powerful Lessons in Personal and Professional Change.*

"Not exactly a book I've been longing to read," he grimaced, swiveling his head in my direction. He added, "Thank you sooo much, Sarah."

"It wouldn't hurt you to read it, Clayton," I scolded. "You could become more organized and focused instead of always operating on sheer faith and optimism. The way you do things gives everyone ulcers," I said critically.

"Now, Sarah, you'll be pleased to know that this time I will be able to make my semi-annual mortgage payment on time."

"And, how did you accomplish that, Clayton?" I questioned.

"Just born under a lucky star, I guess." He smiled.

"I guess that makes everything all right then, Clayton. In fact, I can feel my ulcers healing already."

I sat silently, gazing into the fire, as Clayton regaled us with tales. I remembered that long ago summer when, after completing law school, he realized that he lacked the desire to become a practicing attorney and headed for the mountains of northern Arizona. The mountains seemed to be his passion. He discovered that his heart belonged there. With true entrepreneurial spirit, Clayton acquired an old metal building and converted it into the liveliest restaurant and saloon in town. For many successful years, he operated Bucking Broncos, a charming western establishment that offered live entertainment and was equipped with its own mechanical riding bull. Then, even getting more rural, he sold that business and ventured to Sinagua Basin, an area near Cactus Lake and the tiny rustic community of Cornflower Corners nestled in the mountains, where wild corn once grew. It became his home and his dream.

Designating the name of the town, and displayed for all to see, was a huge yellow sign illuminated with the face of a smiling corncob and decorated with all sorts of blue cornflowers. It was a landmark in itself, serving as a beacon to attract tourists and lost souls alike. And lost souls there were…

It was the type of small town that many see as a refuge. Its "business district" mainly consisted of a post office and a bar, the latter in danger of collapse from the weight of the animal heads hanging on the walls.

It came as no surprise to learn that Clayton now owned that bar and the historic Cornflower Corners Store and Steakhouse. As a well-respected member of the community, he continued to operate various businesses on the main street of that rural setting.

When not playing the role of "Indian Trader," he resided there, surrounded by hills where cattle grazed, occasionally making their way to town—the type of place where it is not unusual to find real cowboys and to see a horse or two hitched to a post out front.

With the wrappings and bows cleared, Clayton walked to the head of the dining room table and sat down as the boys helped Mother and me. After everyone was seated, we sat in quiet reverence as Preston lowered his head, his voice softening as he spoke. "Thank you, Lord, for having blessed us with joys of the richest kind—not wealth, fame or power—but contentment, peace of mind, friendship, and family. Amen!" After we thanked God for His many blessings, we began the feast.

"This is exquisite," Mother commented, taking a bite of the squash soufflé. "Everything is perfect, Sarah."

Everyone agreed. We talked throughout dinner. The boys had been attending separate colleges at the time and couldn't wait to discuss their achievements.

Clayton leaned forward in his chair, "You did a good job, Sarah," he said, while continuing to look at his nephews. I could see by the expression on his face that vivid memories were flashing through his mind.

Usually at family get-togethers, we reminisced about old times. Clayton loved to tell stories, and the way he always told stories was such a hoot. Mother and I moved to the kitchen to get dessert ready as Clayton began, "Let me tell you about the time…"

From the kitchen, I could hear Clayton talking to the boys. "My eyes are getting heavy. They are being drawn back to the small figures dashing along the creek with their pet boxer running in mad circles after them, to the time when you and your mother had joined me at the cabin to visit for the weekend. Yes," he said, "it's all coming back. I remember how I had decided to surprise each of you boys with a brand new fishing pole.

"But, before the day was over…" he paused, "I still wince, remembering how Preston came running into the house shrieking; piercing shrills trailing in the air as he ran. 'Mommy! Mommy! My pole is gone.' His voice reached such high decibels not even a mother could stand the annoying sound. You would have thought he'd been attacked by a bear," Clayton said, as they all laughed.

"Please, go on, Uncle Clayton; I can't wait to hear *your* version of the story," Preston urged.

"…'I'm sorry, Uncle Clayton, that I lost my new pole,' Preston cried out, as the words trembled on his lips and reverberated in the air. But with the look of devastation in his eyes, the tears flowing down his cheeks, and a bewildered expression, Preston found himself being comforted rather than chastened, probably just to keep him quiet," Clayton mumbled.

"But, here comes the kicker! I'm sure you remember the humorous side to this whole fiasco, don't you, Conner? You remember how, earlier, when you spotted the pole unattended, rather than picking it up, you ran all the way back to the cabin to tell Preston. I can still see the anxious expression on your face as you entered the room, blurting the words and gasping breathlessly between. 'Preston! You're gonna be in big trouble. You left your fishing pole down at the creek.' I remembered thinking at the time, 'Now, that's a smart kid!' I'll never forget how Preston, who usually vibrated with restless energy just stood there, paralyzed, in that moment of realization… Sometimes it's difficult to imagine that either one of you kids, much less both, have such high IQs," he concluded teasingly.

We lingered at the table after dessert and listened to music softly playing *Silent Night*. We enjoyed the warmth and wonder that is Christmas as we watched the glow of the firelight, and smelled the sweet fragrance of juniper berries. Comfortably seated by the fire, Clayton and I continued to talk as Mother busied herself tidying up. The boys retreated to the den to play Nintendo games.

I immediately jumped on Clayton as soon as everyone was out of earshot. "Tell me more about the murder of Deputy Morgan's son." I got the distinct feeling that Clayton was about to tell me something, but he hesitated. Perhaps because it was Christmas.

"I have to go now, Sarah," Clayton said softly, as though he didn't want Mother to hear.

"Oh! Stay a little longer," I coaxed. I didn't want to end the celebration that had lasted long after dinner.

"I'd like to, but I can't, Sarah," he said, as he stood to leave. "Bye, kids," he called out. "Keep up the good work. And thanks for the gifts."

"Goodbye, Uncle Clayton," they chimed in unison. "And thanks for yours."

"You're not leaving already, are you?" Mother asked, pleading with him to stay as we walked with Clayton to his truck.

Mother, who was sensitive to the subtle nuances of his deeper feelings, noticed something hidden in his soft eyes. "Goodbye, Clayton," she said, hugging him tightly. "Please heed your sister's warning and be careful up on that reservation," she urged.

"Love you, Clayton," I whispered, as I flung my arms around his neck, kissing his cheek lightly.

"I love you, too," he said, shrugging almost in embarrassment.

My arms loosened from his neck as I looked at his smiling face. If only he knew what he meant to me. He was the best brother a sister could ever have.

As I stood in the open doorway and waved goodbye, I couldn't wait until the next time I saw him.

CHAPTER IV

With the holidays past, it was already more than a week into the New Year. My sons had returned to college and the house was empty. My marriage to their father, a well-established tax attorney and bank executive, ended in divorce when they were just toddlers. I was getting accustomed to the loneliness and found that I didn't mind it quite so much.

It was Monday. Looking out the window, I noticed the winter sun trying to sneak through the gray, cloudy haze. At the time, I was in the insurance business and annuities were offering a whopping ten percent return. The phone rang while I was sitting at the table planning my appointments for the week. As I grasped the receiver, I heard an unfamiliar voice on the other end of the line.

"Is this Sarah Simms, Clayton Conway's sister?" the voice inquired.

"Yes, it is," I replied, my spine prickling at the concern in his voice.

"This is Jerome Kramer, Clayton's new partner at the trading post. I just got a disturbing phone call from Susan Martin," he said seriously. "She's the lady who manages one of Clayton's businesses in Cornflower." His words were adding to the uneasiness that already stirred within me.

"Somebody from the Phoenix Police Department, I think his name was Bennett, contacted Sue at the bar yesterday. He was trying to find Clayton or a relative of Clayton's. Since Sue didn't have your number and you're not listed in the phone book, she called me. Unfortunately, she wasn't able to reach me until this morning," he added nervously. "I guess the cops found your brother's truck abandoned somewhere in Phoenix and your brother was nowhere to be found. I really don't know anything more than that. Just call Sue, she has the information," he said anxiously.

I immediately dialed the number to the Cornflower Corners Store. Reason told me not to panic, but every sense registered danger as I waited, listening to the phone ring. Eventually, Susan Martin answered and explained.

Clayton's vehicle had been found at about three o'clock in the morning in a rough Phoenix neighborhood with crack houses on every corner.

The truck's windows were rolled down, the keys in the ignition, and blank checks strewn on the front seat.

It's impossible! It can't be Clayton's truck. I shuddered. Where is Clayton? My pulse beat furiously upon hearing the sketchy details. I reached Officer Bennett of the Phoenix Police Department. He substantiated what Sue had told me. My brother's truck had been found abandoned. He advised me that I should make arrangements to have it picked up.

"We discovered it early Saturday morning from a 'tip' called in by a local resident," he said. "It does look suspicious," he admitted. "Nobody would leave an expensive truck like that parked in that neighborhood, especially in the condition in which it was found, unless they wanted it to be stolen," he continued, relating the anonymous caller's comment.

"Legally, I'm unable to have it towed," he said in response to my question, "but we will keep it under police surveillance until you arrive."

I called Clayton's home phone number over and over, hoping to hear his voice with each ring. There was no answer. I just knew something dreadful had happened to my brother.

"In the name of God, where could Clayton be?" the tormented voice in my mind repeatedly inquired. I groped for an answer, trying to comprehend. My lungs began to work faster and faster. Gasping in shallow, rapid breaths, I realized that I had begun to hyperventilate. Desperately trying not to panic, I breathed in slowly. A wave of terror washed over me, completely drowning out all reason. I frantically searched my purse for my keys. A huge lump congealed in my throat. Tears welled up in my eyes, making it difficult to see. I rushed blindly toward the door. The phone rang. I ran back and quickly grabbed the receiver.

"I'm sorry!" the voice said apologetically. "This is Officer Bennett again. I don't know how to tell you this, Mrs. Simms, but the truck, while under police surveillance, has disappeared," he said.

"How could this possibly happen?" I asked. But he made no attempt to justify or defend his department's actions. He just hung up.

I realized that Clayton's vehicle was the least of my concerns, for it appeared that not only was Clayton's truck missing, so was Clayton.

Despairingly, I sat alone at the table for several minutes, unable to sort out my thoughts. My heart was beating heavily. What should I do? I repeated the words over and over in my mind.

I agonized over whether or not to tell Mother the distressing news. I had always tried to shield her from bad news, hard decisions, and even the risks of everyday life. As I painfully deliberated, I realized that if the situation were reversed I would definitely want to know. I slowly picked up the phone.

Immediately, Mother could tell by my solemn greeting that I was upset. "What's wrong, Sarah?" she asked.

Trying to mask the worries and doubts that raged in my mind I asked, "Would you mind coming over this morning, Mother? I think I'm going to need your help."

A great weariness crept over me. My knees gave out. I sank into the chair. I stared in rigid silence and waited.

"Mother…" I said softly when she arrived. My mouth was dry. Too dry to speak. Eventually, swallowing hard, I began to tell her the dreadful news and circumstances. "I don't know what to think, Mother," I said, trying to conceal the alarm in my voice, "but it doesn't look good. I know that Clayton wouldn't have left his truck parked in that type of neighborhood—at least not voluntarily."

She stared at me for a moment with incomprehension. "You don't think something happened to him, do you?"

Then Mother's eyes grew stark with urgency. Her lips pressed together as her face twisted in a spasm of pain. "Oh, no!" she cried. I was silent as I saw her fear and felt her anguish. I didn't know what to say. Tears seeped from the corners of my eyes as I watched her suffering.

Officer Bennett had informed me that this case was not within the jurisdiction of the Phoenix police. The FBI usually handled "missing person" cases on the reservation. So, I made an appointment with the FBI for that same day. I drove with Mother to the FBI building, arriving in the early afternoon.

The FBI building was located less than a mile from downtown. After parking in a nearby lot, we paused on the opposite side of the broad street and looked diagonally across at the solid, almost bank-like respectability of the facade. The building was not very lofty, consisting of only four floors, but it had clearly been built at considerable expense and was fairly new. A short flight of steps led up to an imposing main entrance, to one side of which was a massive granite panel with the name of the Bureau incised deeply and impressively in large letters, legible even at this distance.

The soft, calming colors on the walls and the soothing mauve tones of the carpet did little to dispel my fear and anxiety. Having to furnish proof of identification, we showed our drivers' licenses at the window. An arm reached out to collect them. We finally gained access after our identity was established and they determined that we were not carrying concealed weapons. We were introduced to a woman who sat calmly studying us from across her desk.

The FBI woman began to exchange toneless rhetoric with her superior; eventually they determined that they "lacked jurisdiction." But their conclusion seemed incomplete somehow. I wondered if my former husband's entanglement with both federal and state income tax authorities had something to do with their decision. My spirits faltering, I sat bent over in the chair, depressed. It was apparent that the FBI was completely disinterested in this case. "I'm sorry," she said, "but your situation falls entirely out of our jurisdiction. There haven't been any violations of federal laws that the FBI is charged with enforcing," she continued. "Because a non-Indian is involved, we cannot intervene."

"But how do you know an Indian wasn't involved in his disappearance?" I questioned. "Just because Clayton is Anglo…"

"That's just it," she interrupted. "We don't know. From what you have told me, it does appear that your brother could have been abducted, but nothing more is really certain. There have been no ransom demands as yet, no body found, and no signs of struggle."

"Clayton is missing," I blurted emphatically, sensing she doubted the urgency of my plight. "And I can assure you of one thing," I said sharply, with my anger deepening. "He is not basking on a beach somewhere in Mexico.

"Something horrible has happened to him. I just know it. The fact that his truck was found in that type of neighborhood triggers all kinds of alarms to me. Clayton would never leave his truck unlocked under any circumstance, much less leave the keys in the ignition and his windows open, especially in that part of town. He is anti-drugs. He doesn't smoke, and he rarely drinks. It should be obvious that foul play is a factor here," I said, harshly venting my anger.

I knew I was babbling. The woman looked sympathetic, but said nothing.

"This is my understanding. Please correct me if I'm wrong," I said, frustrated. "The Phoenix police are claiming lack of jurisdiction because, although his truck was found here, he was discovered missing from his business on the reservation. According to them, a Missing Person Report can only be filed from the point of origin where the person was discovered missing. Now you're telling me, although the reservation is in your bailiwick and it is the point of origin, that the FBI cannot claim jurisdiction because Clayton is non-Indian. Then, *WHO* has jurisdiction?" I demanded.

As I saw that I was getting nowhere, tears of hopelessness began to burn behind my eyes. I lowered my chin and gave myself a silent order not to cry as I began writing the names of the authorities and agencies that she suggested I contact.

"You might try the Apache County Sheriff's Office. But first I would encourage you to contact the Navajo Tribal Police in Window Rock and the Bureau of Indian Affairs. Good luck," she said in a conciliatory tone.

By now, despair had consumed both Mother and me. How I wished that I had the power to find Clayton, but all I had was a feeling of helplessness. Even though I planned to contact the people on the list of names she had given me, I began to have grave doubts that I would ever see my brother again. I sighed in tired desperation as we arrived home. That night, overwhelmed by the rush of thoughts, my mind was in agony. Moving closer to the bed, I sank to my knees beside it. As the tears welled in my eyes and began to flow down my cheeks, I prayed, desperately pleading to God to help me…begging Him for a miracle.

With my glazed eyes still fixed on a distant star that was shining brightly through the window, my thoughts turned to that remote trading post, that mystical place of gods and of destiny. I had been given a forewarning, the gift of sight, and I hadn't realized it. I hadn't listened, although I heard the spirits of dead men, their voices restless in the wind.

Consciously, with all my senses, I intently listened to the inner voice within me. The tears filled the deepness of my heart as I wept quietly inside. I shrank from the thought of telling the boys—afraid that if I voiced my greatest fear, it would come true.

Before going to bed, I walked in numb silence to the room where Mother was staying. Reaching out for comfort, I clutched her to me, trying to soothe her troubled heart as well. Her ashen face was a hard mask of pain. Reflected from her eyes was intense fear.

Alone in my room, a cold lump of fear still swelled in my chest as my head touched the pillow. With my eyes fixed on the ceiling, I watched the empty darkness. At first, I saw only the blackness. Then, strange shapes and figures began to take form. I lay open-eyed in an absorbed trance-like state. In this altered state of consciousness I could see dark forms that were deadened a deep black in the gray light, slowly becoming hazily distorted to black-hooded silhouettes. Wavering silently, the fragments stirred.

Suddenly leaping into clarity, four hooded forms leaned forward and bent to look down into the dark depths of an abyss that I could not recognize. In the starkness of the night, the shape of a windmill towered ominously behind the figures. I tried to interpret what I was seeing and what I felt. Was it a vision? A kind of wakeful dream? As I stared at the haunting shapes that hovered above, my eyelids began to flutter in terror with the realization that I was seeing through Clayton's eyes.

I screamed a voiceless scream. Then I bolted upright, momentarily paralyzed by the awareness. Disoriented and still in a trance, my eyes remained fixed and staring. I tried to recapture the vision, but the air, solid as stone, would not let me through. Weary, drained of all thought and feeling, I collapsed back down onto the bed. Lowering my lids, I began to feel reality slipping away. I finally sank into a deep sleep. I woke early to the quiet darkness of the room. Had I experienced a paranormal revelation? In the past, I had a few isolated experiences of extra-sensory perception, although I would not consider myself psychic.

Chapter V

Mother sat with her hands clasped in front of her and looked straight ahead, as if focusing on some distant horizon. We had left early, before the dawn broke, expecting to be hampered by bad weather once we reached the high country. The Navajo Nation, according to the news, was about to experience the worst winter storm of the season. Humbled by a sense of powerlessness, I didn't quite feel my usual "take charge" sort of energy. If only I were a little turtle, I would have tucked myself into my shell and waited for the threat to be over. My only hope was that Mother Nature would protect us.

Yesterday's meeting with the FBI had dampened my spirit, but my resolve was firm. Burying the horrible thoughts deep within myself, I refused to accept a forecast of doom. I tried to separate myself from what was happening. To halt my tears, I resolutely looked at the white lines.

Having made prior arrangements to meet with an attorney in Window Rock, I hoped to bypass the notorious bureaucracy of the Navajo Tribal Police. Jolene, who worked for the Justice Department representing the Navajo Nation, was a long-time friend of Clayton's. Perhaps with her help and through her influence somebody might be more inclined to listen to me, I thought, nourishing the hope.

An hour and a half later, we stopped at a roadside restaurant to eat. We were in some little burg on the outskirts of Flagstaff. Not exactly a quaint place, I thought, as I stepped out of the car onto the snow that dusted the parking lot. I drew in a deep lungful of cold air. Despite the heavy fur jacket I wore, I still felt cold.

After eating in silence, we were on our way again in a short time. We drove steadily as the road led up through stands of thin stunted trees. Looking out at the dormant terrain, I felt emptiness. Shivering, I gazed at the cold bleakness of the frozen earth, seeing no beauty. Undaunted by the weather, my eyes vacantly stared through the furious white flakes that started flying at the windshield. "Please let our efforts be not in vain," I prayed silently.

I tried to focus on driving as the road became perilous with the season's worst blizzard. Snow clung to the windshield. At times, the highway was all but impassable with snarls of jackknifed trucks. Miles clicked away. I drove as on auto-pilot, right-brain driving, until some reality shook my left brain back to sensibility. My hands clenched the steering wheel so tightly that ripples of pain climbed my arms—first into my wrists, then elbows, and finally my shoulders. My head pounded from the tension.

Through the miles, Mother and I had remained quiet. We were each wrapped in our own thoughts. Glancing from the ghost-white blanket that covered the ground to Mother's face, I realized there was little distinction between her color and the freshly fallen snow. As we exited the freeway, I became aware that the glistening snow on the road concealed a thick layer of ice beneath it. Tightening my grip on the steering wheel and traveling less than twenty-five miles per hour to keep the tires from fishtailing, I continued to navigate the flat, lifeless road to Window Rock.

Releasing my breath in a long sigh, I swung the car into an empty parking space. It had been a staggering eight-hour drive. The day was just beginning I thought, rubbing my aching temples. The snow had stopped, but gusts of wind continued to sweep across the snow-covered lot. Starting across the street, I felt the fierce bite as an icy thrust of wind cut through my jacket. Was Mother Nature striking back? Turning to avoid the piercing cold, my eyes focused on the mocha-colored building. It was an unimpressive, rather faceless structure for such a highly esteemed office.

Arm in arm, Mother and I struggled forward through the snow. We discovered an un-shoveled walkway that led us to the entrance of the Navajo Nation Department of Justice. As a female figure brushed past us, I stopped short. Turning, I watched her as she raced across the parking lot. Impulsively, I called out. "You wouldn't happen to be Jolene? Would you?"

"Why, yes! Are you Sarah?" she yelled back. Looking harried, she scurried back to where we were standing.

"Please, follow me," she said, leading us through the doorway of the ordinary building to her equally unimpressive office.

Looking at the placard on her desk, bearing an official seal and the words Assistant Attorney General printed in gold, gave me a sliver of hope. At least this is a beginning, I thought, as I fingered the edges of the metal placard lightly.

Jolene gave us her intense attention. Clearly understanding our urgency and the seriousness of the situation, she earnestly expressed her grave concerns.

"Do you know anyone who might have wanted to harm your brother?" she asked us.

"Not that I'm aware of," I answered. "As far as I know, everybody liked Clayton."

"I know I surely did," she added. "I can't believe Clayton ran off without notifying anyone of his whereabouts, which is not something Clayton would normally do. I can't imagine what has happened to him." She gazed at me with concern.

"I apologize," she said finally, glancing at her watch, "but I must get going. A crisis has come up in Gallup and I have a court appearance in an hour."

She pushed the chair back from her desk. I watched her dark brown hair, cut in an easy-care style, bounce lightly from around her Anglo face.

"I have made arrangements for an associate of mine to accompany you today," she informed us hastily.

Almost as if on cue, a thin, somewhat disheveled-looking man came forward. "This is Mr. Burke," she said. Jolene made the introductions then she held out her hand. "If there is anything…anything at all," she said. Mentioning again her concern for Clayton, she made her exit.

Having expressed our sincere gratitude and not giving up hope, Mother and I started resolutely through the door. Moving in single file, we walked out, the associate attorney trailing behind. Avoiding the main road, we followed him as he drove his pickup truck along the back streets, arriving shortly at a large, austere building. I noticed that the parking lot was solidly lined with pickup trucks, as I looked out the window at the sign that said Navajo Tribal Police Station.

"This is it," he commented matter-of-factly, as he stood waiting for us to get out of the car. There was a bitter chill still in the air, but at least the wind had released its grip on me. I felt a sense of relief.

We followed Burke as he led us up the steps to the entrance of the Navajo Tribal Police Station. My body ached with residual chill. We waited apprehensively inside the stark building where Jolene's associate had instructed us to remain. Having disappeared down the hallway into the deep umbra of the interrelated passageways, he was gone for what seemed to be an eternity.

At last, two figures emerged from the gloomy shadows. Leading the way and moving across the room in slow deliberation, was an important looking Navajo gentleman. His regal manner conjured up images of a Roman emperor. To say that I was impressed would be an understatement. I rose to greet him, shaking his hand warmly, as he introduced himself as Mr. Begay with the Navajo Tribal Police.

He spoke with patient understanding as he led us through a long corridor past dingy little offices and ushered us into a large conference room. Graciously, he motioned Mother and me to the vacant chairs. "Will you wait a few minutes, please?" he asked politely. "I would like to call my assistant in to join us." Closing the double-paneled doors behind him, he left the room. I think Mr. Burke, Jolene's assistant, regretted that he had remained with us. It felt as though we were confined within the deep recesses of a catacomb. Waiting, with fear raging inside me, I mentally reviewed the scant details that I had learned:

Last Friday, January 10, 1992, Clayton had arrived at the trading post at approximately six o'clock in the evening. Camille, the shaman-like Indian woman who told us the Creation Story, was the last person known to have seen him.

He had been seen earlier that morning in Cornflower Corners with a young male, who helped Clayton load two huge freezers into the back of his truck. Apparently, he had stopped to chat with one of the locals and advised that person of his plans to be at the trading post all weekend. He and the person helping him were last seen in Cornflower Corners as they drove out of town.

Informing Camille that he would be staying the weekend, Clayton had asked her to stop by the following morning to pick up her check, which would be ready by then. As she left for home, he indicated that he would be available to cover the store himself for the next few days.

Camille returned on Saturday for her check, as she had been instructed, but said she saw no sign of Clayton. The doors to the trading post were locked and his truck was gone. She had expected him to be there and hadn't brought her keys, so she turned around and walked back home.

On Monday, arriving for work on schedule with her keys, Camille thought it odd to find the large room vault unlocked. All the money kept in the vault was gone. Upon further investigation, she realized that Thursday and Friday's receipts were also missing. I recalled that Clayton had left Cornflower Corners with $10,000 in cash. That was "chicken feed" compared to the $20,000 or more that Clayton normally carried with him because he had been authorized to cash government checks given to each reservation resident every month as income from grazing, mining, logging, and oil drilling on Indian land.

Clayton usually went up to the trading post on the second day of the month, but apparently this month the checks had been late in arriving. If the young man working with Clayton had seen all of that money, he was clearly a likely suspect.

Shuddering, I roused myself from my thoughts.

Mr. Begay returned, bringing with him a slender, rather loose-limbed man. Both Navajos were dressed in the same olive green garb, which looked attractive against the color of their skin. After introducing himself, the younger man, along with his superior, proceeded to be seated. I looked at their watchful faces as they scrutinized me, every word and every gesture a careful study. Deliberately, I calmed myself, but my head was spinning. Everything seemed to go into slow motion as I peeled back the layers of my memory, telling them the facts that I knew. Mr. Begay sat transfixed, as his bespectacled assistant, eyes averted, scribbled furiously in his notebook. I could see that their minds were trying to put together all the pieces as I explained the frightening circumstances.

"And," I said in conclusion, my face severe and determined, "because of this mounting evidence, I am convinced that something terrible has happened to my brother. I am requesting your help."

Holding him with my eyes, I scrutinized Begay, the man in charge of criminal investigation. The smooth texture of the skin on his round, heavy face made him appear a congenial man. As he sat stolidly in his chair, his eyes hinted of a warm generosity. He returned my stare and compassionately searched my face. I felt that he sympathized with the strain I was under.

From across the massive table, I caught the silent looks he gave to his assistant. He then returned his eyes to mine. Frustrated, I gazed at him in silence, unable to guess what he was thinking. My shoulders grew tense. "You must do something!" I bluntly insisted. "I don't believe..." I started to say, but he cut me off.

"We *are* going to do something," he said in a soothing tone, reaching for the stack of notes his assistant had compiled.

"What?" I queried insistently.

My eyes focused on the clean-shaven jaw as I watched him flip through the notes. "I'm going to assign this to our man in Chinle," he said with conviction. "I'll make arrangements to have him meet with you at the Sub-Agency Station there. I will also notify the Apache County Sheriff's Office, which legitimately has jurisdiction and the Bureau of Indian Affairs," he volunteered as an afterthought.

Before disbanding, having already thanked Jolene's associate, who waited patiently during the lengthy meeting, I turned to Mr. Begay. As he took my hand in his, I felt the genuine warmth of his touch and had to suppress a grateful urge to hug him.

Leaving the Tribal Headquarters encouraged, we buckled our seat belts in preparation for the two-hour drive to Chinle. I could see a faint light of hope at the end of the tunnel. Was this hope based on an illusion?

Fear continued to simmer within me, stirring from time to time. "Don't let fear be your thoughts," I whispered to myself. Letting my thoughts drift, my eyes were drawn to the trees standing alone in silence. Stubbornly resistant to destruction, I focused on their tall, sturdy torsos. I realized that our bodies also had special reserves in times of need. Like the trees, we've been given a strength and resiliency, something essential that allows us to persevere. As we continued the drive, I tried to shut out my anxieties.

I was unaware that we had arrived in the town of Chinle until I found myself driving along its Main Street. I searched for the address of our destination and finally came across the red brick building. After parking the car in the small lot adjacent to the main office of the police station, Mother and I stood facing the trailer where the Criminal Investigation unit was located. Carefully crossing the parking lot to avoid the oozing ground of ankle-deep mud, we tiptoed on top of the patches of ice-crusted snow.

Greeting us as we reached the door was a tall, handsome Navajo with magnificent long jet-black hair. Revealing his annoyance at having had to wait for us, his voice was cool and carried no hint of welcome in it. "I'm Sergeant Anton," he said with icy courtesy. "We'll have to make this meeting brief," he said curtly. "It's after six o'clock now."

I watched him move restlessly in his chair, casting his eyes to the clock centered on his uncluttered desk. How I wished it was in my power to turn back the hands of time. I momentarily closed my eyes and asked God to grant my prayer. In answer to the same questions asked by the other agencies, once again I repeated the pertinent facts. Throughout the conversation, I got the distinct impression that this assignment was of little significance to the sergeant.

"Is there anything else?" he asked, anxious to conclude the interview.

Shaking my head slowly in a negative response, my eyes rested critically on him.

"Well, I guess I'll plan to meet you tomorrow morning at eight, if that's okay with you. We'll do a full-scale investigation of the alleged crime scene then," he said. Beneath the surface, his voice was as hollow as the void in his expressionless eyes.

"At the trading post at eight o'clock," I confirmed, feeling a mixture of hope and despair.

"We could eat dinner on the way to the motel if you'd like," I mentioned to Mother, wearily.

"Oh, Sarah. I don't know about you, but I'm almost too tired to eat," she sighed, her body showing signs of fatigue. Seeing her drained face, I drove to the nearest motel, the same one we had stayed in on our first visit to Chinle.

We ate a quick bite in the small coffee shop that adjoined our accommodations and walked back to our room. I slumped into a chair by the door, drained of all thought and feeling, and sat motionless just staring. My mind no longer seemed to work. Of one thing I was certain. I didn't want to go to bed. I was afraid of the nightmares that tormented me. But, I was so tired that I found myself slowly walking toward the bed, wanting to go to sleep.

As soon as my head touched the pillow, I began to think again. As I lay restlessly, staring into the darkness, visions began to flash before my eyes. Once again, I could see the hazy distant black writhing shapes begin to take form. With almost a mystical knowing, my fears all came together as I watched the blackness shaping and reshaping itself into human forms with the windmill in the background. I felt overwhelmed with the realization that I was looking out through the still depths of my brother's soul. I was seeing with a pulsating energy the images of the persons responsible for my brother being in a dark, mortal state of frigid stillness. I continued to toss fitfully for a while then, finally, with my mind blotting the darkness and soaking it up like a sponge, I slept. Later that night, I woke again. I was still questioning myself.

Searching for the answers from within, I thought of how the Indians perceive life. The People (The D*iné*) were born with a deep-rooted faith: faith in nature, in themselves, in their religion, and in their place in the universe, all of which have been molded and strengthened by the land in which they live. Through all runs a vein of continuum. All things are a whole with the spirit as a part of life, not separate from it. Believing that, within humanity is man's soul which mirrors in itself the harmony of the entire world.

According to what Camille once said, "Man has the wisdom that his end is not only in an Afterworld, but in the knowledge of himself." Through this spiritual wisdom he may know and understand the mystery of his Creator.

"Is it a coincidence that their Story contained a flood, an expulsion from one world to the next, and a child suffused in spiritual light…or is it a knowing we are all born with?" I wondered. As I lay thinking about the mysticism blended with our own Christian faith, a journey into my imagination brought me to a medicine wheel. Envisioning myself standing in the middle, hearing the circular rhythm encompassing me, I began to see life in circles—having no beginning and never ending.

I fell asleep; my mind was enveloped in a myriad of emotions—hope, inspiration…fear.

Chapter VI

The first thing the next morning, Jerome Kramer, my brother's partner, arrived as promised at our motel at precisely seven o'clock. Aware that the snow made a four-wheel drive vehicle essential to make it up the hill, he had offered to come get us in his pickup.

'Kramer,' as he was called, was dressed in faded Levis, cowboy boots, and a flannel work shirt. Though the coiling wind blew from the northwest bringing with it an icy chill, he wore no jacket. Tipping his big, black Stetson in greeting, he was not at all what I had expected. Even though a small man, physically unimposing at five-foot six inches and weighing a hundred and thirty pounds, he appeared to be a rough sort, the type you would not want to tangle with. His eyes darted nervously, avoiding contact with mine.

Kramer climbed up into the driver's seat. I opened the passenger door and climbed into the truck, pulling Mother up beside me. While seated together in the front seat, I became aware of an uncomfortable jab against my left thigh. Looking down, I noticed a shiny object. Upon further scrutiny, I discovered that there on the seat, sandwiched between us, was a large gun, the biggest pistol I had ever seen, with its long ominous barrel pointed in the direction of my leg.

"Would you mind removing that?" I asked, glancing at the gun, "or, at least positioning it differently."

Kramer grinned. "Why? Does my gun bother you?"

"Yes, it does," I snapped. "Point it in your own direction, if you insist on having it there."

I viewed him suspiciously as he readjusted the gun's position. Not wishing to antagonize him further, I lightly changed the subject.

"Is there a lot of snow on top of the mountain?" I asked, feeling the unspoken tension.

"Not any deep snow. But there is a storm moving in that should bring heavy snowfall. So, if I were you, I wouldn't plan to stay at the trading post too long." His tone seemed threatening. Or was it my imagination? I didn't relish the idea of being in a vehicle with this man for the next forty-five minutes.

The pickup ascended the steep hill, slowly. The wind thrust its icy fingers through the window that was open barely a crack. Looking out at this uncompromising land, I couldn't help thinking of the abominable spirits that resided here. We reached the summit and the trading post. The snow, piled into high, windblown ridges, dominated the surrounding landscape. Another vehicle was already parked in the lot. I looked at the old fortress. Perhaps this was the destiny that God gave to Clayton. Getting out of the car, I glanced at the familiar juniper tree that loomed grotesquely in the corner. In a state of bent submission, it had finally been subdued by the elements. As I stood there, I could still hear the howls of the *Chindi* behind me in the shadows.

Somehow, my mind was a complete blank about the layout of the trading post as we filed through, progressing from chamber to chamber. Upon entering the store, I could see the slow moving sergeant out of the corner of my eye. Once inside, I noticed a stout gentleman, dressed in a brown uniform, who was talking with Camille. I watched him as he sank his teeth into a large, green apple, the juice streaming down his chin. He reminded me of a barbecued pig, with a giant apple stuck in his mouth. He came charging over to where we were standing and held out his arm, extending his hand to Mother.

"Let me introduce myself," he said boldly. "John Morgan! Assistant Deputy with the Apache County Sheriff's Department. You must be Mrs. Conway. And you," he paused turning to me, "must be Clayton's sister."

"That's right," I confirmed as I watched him wipe the apple juice off his chin with his sleeve. What a slob, I grimaced.

Having gotten through the formalities of introduction, I began to keenly observe him as he spoke. In contrast to his sloppy appearance, he seemed to be extremely intelligent. He also had an exaggerated way of trying to impress others with his sincerity.

"I've been trying to extract information from Camille, but that has proven to be difficult," he said, sweeping away the wiry hair that kept flopping in his face. "In their religion, it is taboo to speak of the dead."

How do they know he's dead? I thought. Did they know something that I didn't know?

"I'm afraid she is not a very credible witness."

That was an odd statement too. Just because the subject was taboo, did that make Camille less credible?

"From what little information I could get," he grunted, "she described the person last seen with Clayton as a young white male in his late teens or early twenties. He was tall and thin, perhaps a little taller than your brother. Camille thought that he was wearing a dark jacket, a green army jacket, although she wasn't quite sure of the color. In addition to the obvious clues that something wasn't right, Camille has made some further observations since your brother's disappearance. While going through the house, she discovered that the television had been left on and that Clayton's jacket, the one he had last been seen wearing, was lying across the bed. She also found an uncooked steak and some corn that had apparently been set out on the kitchen counter in preparation for dinner. So, if your brother left of his own volition, he left in a mighty big hurry.

"Stranger yet," he added quizzically, "she noted that the tablecloth was missing. In my opinion," he volunteered, "it does appear that foul play could have been a factor. With that much money on him, he would have been a prime target for robbery and murder," he concluded.

I didn't challenge the thought because I had already postulated the same theory. Having had my desperation and fears reinforced, I stood numbly, realizing how precarious life is. At any moment we could find ourselves in peril. We never know when our time on this earth will be over.

With my spirits crumbling, my mind weighed the futility of the situation with increasing urgency. Not wanting to give up, I tried to be optimistic; but with each moment of each hour, I knew the chances of Clayton's being alive were dwindling.

Tears burned behind my eyes as I walked through the vast emptiness of the house. Coming to Clayton's room, I stopped. Inside, sitting forlorn in the dismal loneliness, was his light blue duffel bag, still fully packed. Propped on top was the book, *Powerful Lessons in Personal and Professional Change*, which I had given him for Christmas. Seeing it, the tears exploded. I wept uncontrollably.

On my way back to the kitchen I found both the longhaired sergeant and John Morgan investigating the premises. I observed them engaged in the tedious process of dusting for fingerprints.

Even to the casual onlooker, they appeared sadly incompetent. They took fingerprints off the candlestick on the mantle, the graphite powder so thick it looked like they had plucked the candleholder from an arson scene. And they still didn't get any fingerprints. Almost as if with deliberate intention, significant items were overlooked while they focused on inconsequential things, things that looked as if they hadn't been disturbed in a decade.

"What about this coffee cup over here on the desk?" I asked. Still containing residual remains, it was apparent that it had been left recently. "Clayton usually didn't drink coffee."

"Oh! Don't worry! We'll get to that," John Morgan said.

"And what about this whole trash bag full of pop and beer cans," I said intrusively, pointing to it. Looking inside, I recognized the empty cans of Diet Coke, which Clayton drank regularly. He rarely drank beer.

"We'll take those to the lab," he assured me.

"Did you know Clayton?" I asked, studying him, knowing that I had recognized his name.

"Yes, I did," he responded, not elaborating further.

Volunteering nothing further, he continued with his own agenda. "It's in our hands now," he said conclusively, citing the legal jurisdiction that the Apache County Sheriff had over this matter. "The sergeant here will be assisting our office," he added, exercising his authority. "We have good interagency cooperation, don't we?" He nodded at the sergeant for confirmation, but the Navajo did not support his claim with a return gesture of assurance.

Although Deputy John Morgan did not mention or convey it, I felt he had a social responsibility and a personal one he could not ignore. Having lost his own son to the hands of a brutal murderer right here in this same place, I was hoping he would at least take a special interest in this case, especially since he had been acquainted with Clayton.

I watched him as he took the palm of Mother's hand in his. "I'm sorry," he said gravely, a mournful expression upon his face. "I want you to know I care." I noticed his voice dripped with what seemed to be heartfelt sensitivity.

Something about the way in which the authorities were handling the case bothered me. I went from being skeptical to being cynical, from being irritated to being angry, from being somewhat disillusioned to being completely distrustful. Was his sympathy feigned? It was so easy to trust him, yet so horribly frightening. What if he possessed incompatible motives as yet undisclosed? What if we were to discover an incongruity between his attitude and behavior? Mother already sensed something in this man.

"I promise I'm going to see this to the end," he said with conviction as he walked us to the front door.

Stepping onto the pathway, I tried to soothe my lungs and my mind with the fresh air. Was it a figment of my imagination or was Morgan's manner deceptively friendly? Did I detect a disturbing note of evasiveness in his voice? Could there be reason for him to deliberately conceal something from us? Doubt gnawed at me. Every thought, every nuance, every detail went through my mind as I examined him with distrust and suspicion. The idea that presented itself was absurd. What hidden motive could he possibly have? I dismissed the frightening notion that percolated in my mind and decided to be grateful for all the help I could get.

"Once again, I didn't listen to myself! But why?" I muttered, stubbornly resistant.

I continued to visualize a smiling, vibrant Clayton and would not give way to ugly possibilities as we started driving back over the deeply rutted road. It seemed that there was always a 'glow' surrounding my brother. But, even as I remembered that sunny moment with Clayton looking at me, waving and smiling from the drive in front of the trading post, I knew it was only a wishful vision—something that had vanished. Peering morosely out of the window, I knew this would no longer be a place of fond memories. I could hear it in the moaning trees and see it in the weeping rocks. The day ended gray and cold as Kramer dropped Mother and me off at the motel.

The painful mystery of Clayton's disappearance lay heavily on our minds while we continued to drive in silence. Most of the way home, Mother's face remained expressionless. With her head resting on the back of the seat, I could see her struggling to fight back tears. It was all I could do to suppress mine. It had been more than three turbulent days of breakneck madness, interspersed with numbness and fear. I was glad to be home and glad to be alone, as Mother and I parted. A drink might steady my nerves, I thought, as I went straight to the cabinet where the liquor was kept. Trembling, both from exhaustion and fear, I awkwardly mixed a good stiff drink, two parts Vodka to one splash of Rose's lime juice.

Sitting alone in the living room, I studied the icy depths of my glass. Its chill was not as cold or as deep as the pain inside of me. Swirling the contents, watching it splash against the rim, my mind seemed to whirl like a raft caught in an eddy, its undertow threatening to pull me down under and away from physical and mental health. Almost by instinct, my numb fingers tightened around the glass, as though it were an anchor. Hoping it would ease the pain and enable me to ride out the storm that was coming, I took a large gulp.

Slowly making my way to the bedroom, I turned to look in the hallway mirror. I studied the pale, intense face, eyes sunken and circled. How could I have aged so quickly? I thought, looking at the chiseled marks of anguish sculpted deeply around my mouth. The pitiless light incised every wrinkle, every hair, and every tear. Alone in my room, trying to erase the horrific memory of the past few days, I collapsed onto the bed, exhausted.

As much as I didn't want to tell the boys. It was time…

I picked up the phone and called Preston at his fraternity house at Arizona State University. Preston, during the fall of his sophomore year had been elected president of his fraternity, and would remain so for the next few years. I listened as he told me how he came up through the ranks.

"First, I served as Scholarship Chairman before being elected President, and before you say anything, Mom," he continued quickly without taking a breath, "that had nothing to do with why I was awarded a Leadership Scholarship." He was so excited and proud of his accomplishment that I hated to dampen his spirit.

Tongue-tied, I finally managed to murmur, "That's great!"

"What's the matter, Mom? You don't sound like yourself."

There was a moment of silence.

"I have some disturbing news to share. There's a good probability that something happened to Clayton," I said in a voice that didn't sound like my own. "He's missing. There may even be a possibility that he's dead. A county sheriff's deputy and a tribal police officer are at the Blue Sage Trading Post now, searching for fingerprints and footprints. They don't know what to think, but I suspect there is foul play involved."

"Geez, do you really think that's possible?" He spent the next half-hour trying to console me.

Then, I called Conner at his fraternity house at the University of Arizona. Conner, my computer whiz-kid, as Clayton referred to him, had recently received a scholarship. I began by congratulating him on his academic achievement. He seemed pleased. Then he started to relate his fraternity adventures. "You should see the Mazatlan pictures," I heard him say, as his cohorts laughed in the background.

Taking a deep breath, I said, "I wish I didn't have to tell you this." The knot in my stomach tightened into what felt like a ball of lead. "I believe that something dreadful may have happened to Clayton."

"What? Why?" He sounded shocked and at a loss for words.

I told him what I knew about Clayton's mysterious disappearance.

"I'm sorry, Mom. I know how close you are to Clayton." His voice began to crack.

I started to cry.

Time crawled by with the likely probability of the search petering out altogether. With each phone call, the response was the same.

"There's nothing much we can do Ma'am, until the weather clears up. With all this new snow, if your brother is out there, we wouldn't be able to find him until then."

Having completed one such conversation, I slammed the receiver in its cradle. Just as I went to lift it again for another feeble attempt to recruit the help of the FBI, the phone rang.

"Hello, is this Sarah?" the unfamiliar voice inquired.

"Yes," I said reluctantly, waiting to see if it was one of those annoying marketing calls.

"You don't know me," she began, forming her words in slow, measured tones. "I was a very good friend of your brother."

It seemed a little strange to me that she used the past tense "was," but I made no comment as she went on.

"Perhaps I can offer a different perspective on the case," she said.

What in God's name is she talking about, I wondered?

As she continued, I found out. "I am a psychic and would like to act as a catalyst to help solve Clayton's mysterious disappearance. I have known your brother a long time, although until now, I was unaware that he had a sister."

CHAPTER VII

Admittedly, I was skeptical right from the start. Certainly if the caller had known Clayton for any length of time, she would have known about me. As the conversation progressed, however, I was at least able to ascertain that she wasn't a charlatan eager to exploit the very anxieties she sought to assuage. Further, she didn't seem like the oddball type that generally is attracted to that field, or so I thought, as I pictured the stereotypical tealeaf readers and crystal-ball gazers donned in unusual garb with exotic-sounding names. Then again, her name was Madelyenna, Madelyn for short. Preferring not to discuss matters further over the phone, we both hung up.

Having made arrangements to pick her up and bring her to my home, I was excited by the prospect of having someone who was willing to take an interest. I had heard of psychics being summoned across international boundaries to work on cases. Still, I found it surprising that this lady was offering her assistance, agreeing to act as a consultant and work with the police free of charge.

It was nearly 7 p.m. as I approached the rows of tract homes on the dimly lit side street. Stopping the car in front of the address that was scribbled on my notes, I paused before getting out. Something kept bothering me. Perhaps it was the fact that she didn't know that Clayton had a sister. How absurd, I thought. Everyone knew about me. He always enjoyed relating some of my more dramatic experiences, usually mocking my behavior. I remember it took him almost two months to quit telling the story of how I had two turkeys for Thanksgiving dinner, meaning my ex-husband and current boyfriend. I was always one of Clayton's favorite topics of conversation. Again, the question surfaced. Why? Why didn't he ever mention me to Madelyn? It gnawed at me, especially since he liked to needle me about my psychic intuition.

A stout, rather petulant looking woman stood in the open doorway as I approached the entrance. Somewhere behind that boorish look, there was a very pretty face. But she had such intimidating eyes, I thought, as I observed her. She could stare anyone down.

"I'm ready," she said, clutching her purse, and beginning to discuss her relationship with Clayton as we advanced toward the car.

"He used to frequent a bar that I previously owned," she said nervously. "That was some time ago, when he owned Bucking Broncos. On a slow night, he would come down to my place, The Stetson House, and visit with members of the band. He knew all of them, since they had made the rounds, playing at the local establishments."

"What are you trying to tell me?" I asked curtly. I knew of the cheap, run-down saloon of which she was speaking. It had the reputation of being the wildest, drug-infested place in that town. Having previously spent the better part of one hour convincing the authorities that Clayton was not involved in drugs, perhaps I over-reacted. "Are you implying that Clayton was associated with a bunch of druggies?" I challenged. Even as I said the words, I wondered what Clayton would be doing in such a low life place.

"Oh, no," she said emphatically. "On the contrary, Clayton was always counseling them, encouraging them to get off drugs and get their lives together."

"I'm sorry," I said apologetically, easing the tension. Sitting beside her in the car and looking into those fearsome eyes, I was glad to have made amends. I wouldn't want to cross her.

On the way back to my house, Madelyn expounded on psychic phenomena. While theorizing that everyone had some psychic ability, which could be developed by training, she asserted that ESP is a gift like any other artistic talent.

"A psychic cannot explain the source of his or her remarkable ability any more than a virtuoso pianist or a great painter can," she said. "Some psychics view their talents as divine dispensations and act as 'channelers' from the spirit world, but I take a more naturalistic approach," she said, explaining that she believed her psychic functioning to simply be an extenuation of her natural senses.

"That might be true," I said, remembering my dream. "Although, Madelyn, I'm sure you know that psychic powers have sometimes been considered to be a curse to those unfortunate enough to be plagued with them," I said with authority.

"The idea of the paranormal frightens some people, who believe it to be tinged with the supernatural," she said.

"I'm one of those people," I told her, remembering how I had thrown the Ouija board in the trash can the first time I had used it.

"The ability is not something to fear," she assured me. "Rather than an intrusion or the intervention of a deity or spirit, psychics just think less analytically. They use and develop their right brain, which, according to biological theories is the part of the brain that is the seat of creativity, intuition, and pattern recognition. Telepathy, for example, is direct mind-to-mind communication. Clairvoyance is knowing about something somewhere else in space, tapping into a 'universal mind' if you will. Precognition is knowing about the future. Retro-cognition, which is primarily where my thoughts will be focused, is looking backward in time."

"The saddest part of this whole thing..." She paused, her face collapsing into an expressionless void. "I remember having had a glimpse into the future before this tragedy occurred. I had a vision of not only his destiny, but mine too," she said in a melancholy tone. "I tried to forewarn Clayton..."

Instantly, I made the connection. "So, you're the lady who was supposed to work at the trading post?" I commented, although not entirely surprised by the revelation. She certainly looked like she could handle herself just fine up there, I thought. What a huge discovery this was! I never believed that I would meet this woman.

Having established her credibility, I felt my defenses begin to slip away. Although my guard was down, I didn't completely drop my shield. There was still that question of why Clayton hadn't told her about his sister. That puzzled me.

Arriving at my front door, fumbling to unlock it, I began to have second thoughts. Could Madelyn have had something to do with my brother's disappearance? Nevertheless, I entered. As she followed, I ushered her into the kitchen.

Turning to face her, I observed her deep hypnotic eyes. "Would you like something to drink?" I asked edgily.

"Water would be fine," she answered, nervously glancing around the room.

"Please, go ahead and sit down," I motioned, as she seated herself in the chair across the table from mine.

"Don't think me rude, but I'd like to get this over with," she said, urging me to sit down also.

"Psychics re-live the event," she began. "We can experience the pain, emotional trauma, and even the death of the victim. Some psychics say they get visions of the crime from the eyes of the victim."

Strange she should say that, I thought, because that's exactly the way I feel, whenever I experience that dark vision. It's almost as if I were looking up from the bowels of the earth, seeing through my brother's eyes.

"But instead," she continued, "I link my mind with that of the victim's, as if I were standing beside him," she stated, assuming a more confident posture.

Sitting immobile at the kitchen table, I listened as she began to open the doors on the past. What would we find behind them? I shuddered with anxiety. Was I really prepared to know?

There was a pervasive calm in the room. The atmosphere seemed unnaturally still. With her hands clasping her temples and her eyes drawn tightly closed, her breathing slowed to an almost imperceptible rhythm. I watched as her head fell slightly back, resting against the wall. I could see the lids of her eyes twitch and her body go limp, succumbing to what appeared to be an unconscious state.

"There is a room with a desk in the middle of a long house," Madelyn began, recreating the crime scene and describing it in perfect detail.

She related everything she saw as if she stood next to him. Then she told me, "Someone comes to the front door, someone Clayton knows. He is surprised to see him. Suddenly, Clayton realizes that there is a sawed-off shotgun pointed at his face…and another gun, a pistol," she added. "Recognizing his potentially vulnerable situation, he tries to get away, but he cannot escape. Before he can get to the door, two men bring him back, forcibly sitting him down at the kitchen table."

I listened, unable to make a sound. Every muscle in my body tensed as she spoke. My clammy, chilly flesh now seemed to burn as the heat flushed my face and limbs. The effect it had on Madelyn was tenfold, I noticed, as I looked at her glistening, sweat-bathed face. Although appearing to be in a deep sleep, her body seemed to have a sudden awareness. As I continued to watch, the breathing in Madelyn's chest became rapid. Her neck vein pulsed faster. I knew she was reaching the critical moment when she would actually visualize the crime.

"An argument ensues," she said. She started to say something else and then stopped. Suddenly, her eyes flashed wide open, wild with panic and fear.

"There is shock and terror on Clayton's face," she said, her eyes fixed and staring. "Then there is a huge exploding sound of gunfire."

She flinched, and in that moment of dreadful silence, I knew she had witnessed something terrifying. "The other man pushed Clayton's head down on the table with his pistol and pulled the trigger, fatally shooting him."

As if deafened by the noise, she sat silently. I could see the wrenching pain on her face. The pain that Clayton must have felt as the shot, the blast that sent the bullet crashing through his head, penetrated his skull, exploding all thought and feeling.

A sinking feeling pierced my heart as I pictured his slumping body thrust forward, helpless and lifeless. Holding onto the burning image of my brother's face and eyes, I felt the heat flood through my head as though I myself had been shot. It was as if the gates of hell had opened. I looked deep into its exploding fires. What sort of person would commit such a crime? Or was it a person? Then the symbolism hit me. Could there have been a connection between the deaths that occurred at the trading post and its black aura? Did the *Chindi* have anything to do with it? Could they have been responsible for my brother's murder?

I shuddered. Could Madelyn have really seen my brother's death in her psychic vision—before it had happened? Did she have advance warning that Clayton would be killed and that she would be killed also if she went to work at the trading post? According to what Clayton told Mother, the reason this lady gave for not showing up was that she had some "notion" that they both would be killed.

She quoted his flippant response. "In case you are correct, Madelyn, please let me know beforehand, before it happens, before my time runs out."

I sat immobilized by the image of Clayton's violent death.

"Are you all right?" Madelyn blurted, interrupting my thoughts.

"Yes," I sighed, still feeling horror, but detaching from the graphic scene as I tried to find some rationality. "It's just difficult to accept the cruelty in the world. But more importantly, how are you Madelyn? This has to be an enormous strain on you. I recall that you had a premonition before and told Clayton he was in danger." Without making any verbal response, she continued.

She told me that this was a well-conceived plan…four people were involved and it definitely was a conspiracy. This was a premeditated act. It was not spontaneous," she said with conviction. "Theoretically, this is not your usual murderer. This person was motivated by greed and power. This involved elaborate planning and was executed in a calculated manner, so as to minimize risks."

I sat listening, mouth agape, not taking so much as a breath as she proceeded to profile the killer.

"This line of reasoning leads me to deduce that the mastermind is an 'organized offender,' one who has mental clarity of mind. He will do everything possible to prevent identification either of the victim or of himself. He may wipe away fingerprints from the entire scene of the crime, wash away blood, and move or conceal the body. The longer the victim remains unidentified, the greater the likelihood that the crime will not be traced back to its perpetrator."

I shrugged. I didn't have to be a psychic to figure that out. What criteria would she use to determine a "disorganized offender?"

"But they didn't know about you," she said. A hint of a smile lifted her otherwise severe-looking face. "Nor did they count on your ability to penetrate the bureaucratic bullshit of the Navajo Tribal Police," she said in a crude, although accurately descriptive manner. "It is a tribute to your unrelenting efforts that an investigation was underway in just a few days."

Still choked with shock and abhorrence, I nodded, acknowledging her compliment.

"There is something they want," she continued, her eyes closing in deep meditation. "They believe you have some papers, incriminating papers, in your possession. Something to do with business. Yes. A business transaction," she affirmed. "You could be in grave danger yourself.

"I suggest you notify everyone that you no longer have any books or records…that your lawyer has all of Clayton's paperwork. In the meantime, we can put together a paper trail and try to pinpoint who had a motive." She leaned over the table closer to me. "Don't trust anyone," she cautioned. "In fact, someone might try to interject himself into the investigation. Not only do I think that you might be in danger, I feel that you may be getting set up. But whatever their plans, remember they are methodical killers. They took great care to avoid leaving any clues. If their design is to eliminate you, they will probably make it look like a suicide or an accident," she warned.

"Don't worry; I don't trust anyone," I said, facing her glare. There was something definitely frightening about her and those deep, black, penetrating eyes.

Claiming to have "seen" spiders in a deep hole or cave, she pronounced that his body would be found in or near water. She felt that the kid who was helping Clayton haul the equipment was definitely involved, that he was a plant. She theorized that he was the one who drove Clayton's truck to Phoenix on January 12th, not on the 11th as the original police report indicated. Then again, the police report was only as good as the anonymous tipster's statement, which was unverifiable. She concluded that there were two vehicles involved and that the occupants of those vehicles followed one another, caravan style, spending the night in Payson—one party continuing on to Phoenix and the other returning to Cornflower Corners.

After the almost two-hour session, we were both ready to call it a night. Madelyn had excused herself from the room. Meanwhile, I sat dazed with my head pulsing. She was gone for what seemed an awfully long time.

"I'm ready to leave now," Madelyn said, upon returning to the kitchen. I wearily extracted myself from the chair. Again, there was that feeling of everything revolving in slow motion as I walked with her to the door and accompanied her to the car.

Outside, the stars sparkled against the distant sky. Searching the heavens with my welled-up eyes I stared at the luminous universe. If Madelyn was correct, then God, in His infinite wisdom must have had a purpose for taking Clayton. But, why? I asked, pleading for understanding.

The drive back to Madelyn's home seemed long. Again, she cautioned me to be careful. "I feel you could be in grave danger," she warned. "Is there someone who can stay with you?" she inquired, not waiting for an answer. "Do you have an alarm? Do you have a dog? Do you have a gun?"

Having answered "no" to all of her questions, a sudden fear came over me. What if she was right? I didn't want to think about it.

Although there was no way to confirm her psychic vision until the real killer(s) were unmasked, there was no plausible explanation for her uncanny certainty. I didn't know for sure if I had completely believed her as she told of a conspiracy to murder; however, I did know that she had never been to the crime scene. In that respect, she surely hit the mark.

Was it mere chance that her vision coincided with mine that we both interpreted our extended perception to mean he was in a deep hole? Was I molding my memories of the dark-hooded forms in my vision to conform to her prophecy? Should I pursue a psychic's hypothesis? Or thoroughly denounce it? Madelyn had warned that harm could come to me. Was she setting me up? While pondering the answers, the ominous possibility remained. I realized that my life actually could be in danger.

After stopping the car in front of Madelyn's home, I watched her Reubenesque form as she disappeared behind the arched facade. Sitting alone in the car, my mind replayed our bizarre meeting. All of a sudden, the memories flooded back, the image of Clayton. Never had I envisioned that my brother, my only sibling, would die a violent death. Had I really witnessed tonight how he had struggled and died? Feeling close to despair, I found myself pushing down on the accelerator. I just wanted to get home.

CHAPTER VIII

The search for Clayton, or his body, continued. The authorities were re-examining the buildings and grounds at the trading post, in hopes of finding some clue that would explain what happened to him.

"His disappearance baffles us," John Morgan confessed. "Clayton had some huge debts, but, as you stated, he was resolving those. I just don't know..." he said, trying to discern a motive for my brother's mysterious disappearance.

"It's conceivable that there was foul play, but nothing has been disturbed," he continued in a puzzled voice, as he and Clayton's new business partner stood in the open doorway of the trading post.

I kept playing over the possibilities in my mind. Perhaps he had been kidnapped. Even as the thought formed, it evaporated. I thought about the windmill standing alone, but they had searched the property with a "fine-toothed comb," they told me.

"Let's face it," Morgan said. "If there was foul play, that kid who was helping Clayton was probably the culprit."

Mother, who had been wandering aimlessly, followed behind me as I walked with John Morgan into the kitchen. Seated at the table, we continued our conversation, trying to determine a motive other than the obvious. In examining every possibility, I mentioned knowing that several long-time employees had been let go when Clayton took over the operation of the trading post. They were later re-hired at the behest of Clayton's new business partner. I was aware that, in one instance, a heated argument ensued with barbed words flowing bitterly from the mouth of one Navajo man.

However, my insinuation drew an emphatic response from John Morgan. "It was not Lenny, and I know Wilbur would not have confronted Clayton," he declared.

"How can you be so sure?" I questioned, puzzled.

His answer was vague. Stressing that he had known both men a long time, he further attempted to convince me that they had absolutely no involvement in Clayton's disappearance. "This is a White Man's war, not an Indian's war. Besides, they wouldn't lie."

"Well, it's obvious that someone around here has been lying, or as the Indians say, 'speaking with a forked tongue'...or Clayton wouldn't be missing!" I said, staring him in the eye. "Somebody Clayton must have trusted." Having been advised earlier that Lenny and Wilbur were cousins to Camille, I had the feeling that they all shared some sort of relationship besides kinship. What I didn't know was how Morgan fit into the picture.

I felt there was evasiveness in his manner. Something I couldn't quite put my finger on as I watched him move uncomfortably in his chair.

Willfully choosing to disregard his vague answer, I proceeded to tell him of an unfortunate situation that had happened to Clayton a few months back.

"Richard, the man who was managing the trading post for Clayton at that time, allegedly misappropriated a large sum of money. It wasn't until Clayton began receiving bills for thousands of dollars worth of merchandise that should have already been paid, that he uncovered the discrepancies in the books. He confronted Richard and fired him, threatening to expose him to the authorities if he didn't make restitution. This man, Richard Morrison, I believe was his last name, at least made an effort to make amends, giving Clayton title to an old dilapidated trailer as partial payment, along with an accompanying letter of apology, which included a promise to pay the remainder owed."

No sooner had I finished my last statement than I heard the telephone ring, a jarring sound as it echoed in the emptiness.

"Make sure you find out who's calling and why," Morgan called out. "Be sure to get the names and telephone numbers of all callers," he said with authority.

I watched as Kramer moved quickly to answer the phone. "It's Richard Morrison," he yelled loudly.

Dismissing the call, John Morgan yelled back. "Yeah, he used to work here. You can disregard that call, Kramer."

Apparently, it didn't take long for the incongruity to register as Mother's mind caught on those words. As soon as Morgan left the table, she leaned over and whispered quietly to me. "Didn't you find it odd, Sarah, that John Morgan wasn't the least bit concerned when Richard Morrison called? I couldn't believe that he never even inquired as to why he was calling, especially after we had just discussed the fact that this fellow, Richard, might have had a possible motive."

"Yes, Mother. How ironical. It disturbed me as well." I was absolutely sure that Morgan was not telling us everything.

John Morgan returned shortly.

"Didn't you used to own the trading post?" I inquired, the connection suddenly occurring to me.

"Yes, I did. That was before your brother took it over." His answer was brief and constrained.

"Personally, I think that anyone who worked at the trading post should be considered a suspect in my brother's disappearance, even Camille," I said, beginning to compile a list of possible suspects.

"Camille may be an employee here, but do you really think she belongs on a list of suspects? I mean, physically, that petite woman couldn't hurt a fly. Besides, she is sort of a shaman," explained Morgan.

"She knows something," I said. "I'm sure of it. We can't rule out anyone," I insisted.

"I doubt she knows anything more than what she has already told us," Morgan retorted. "But right now, we're looking for someone who has a possible motive, so we can cross her off, and of course, myself."

"Why you?" I asked.

"Because I know I didn't do anything to your brother. If you want to keep my name on *your* list, that's your privilege, but I'm not on mine."

"What about Camille's cousins?" I asked. "Couldn't there have been collusion?"

"Between any of those three? Never. Too unimaginative, too apathetic, and too uncertain of each other's loyalties."

They seemed pretty loyal to me.

He looked over and whispered to me, "I was thinking more along the lines of Kramer."

"Jerome Kramer? Clayton's new business partner? I wouldn't put anything past him. He's a snake."

"If you shake hands with Kramer," Morgan said, "count your fingers afterwards. He's a sly one and so is his daughter, Bobbie Jo."

Later in the morning, I was still at the trading post, frantically searching for clues, when out of the blue I heard Camille's voice.

"There is a Star Gazer who needs to talk to you," she announced, as she barged into the office.

"A what?" I responded, puzzled. I hadn't a clue what she was talking about.

"He is a medicine man," she explained. "He can 'see' keenly, see visions."

"I don't have time for that now, Camille," I said, in an effort to dismiss her.

Undeterred, she stepped back, allowing him to enter.

Although he had expressed an urgent need to speak with me, once inside, he seemed reluctant to do so in front of Camille.

"There are things that have happened at this trading post," he said, hesitating. "Things that have happened in the past. I must warn you…"

Warn me? About what, I wondered. I was speechless.

His expression was one of alarm, "…about the *Chindi*," he said in a half whisper, "about the spirits who do not rest. There is a curse…The Curse of the *Chindi*," he continued, his unblinking eyes penetrating mine.

Why wasn't I surprised? Clayton had once told me that the Indians believed that the trading post was haunted. "A place haunted by its own past," if I recalled his words correctly. At the time, I thought he was just joking. I shivered as I listened to the monotonous voice.

The Star Gazer leaned in a little closer. "A long time ago…on a sultry night…at the end of a dark, lonely road, there was a murder." Without going into detail, he told me the weirdest story about a tiny infant who was crushed to death by his father's huge hands, and of its mother, who wailed, 'My baby is dead, my baby is dead. You've killed my baby.'"

"Whose baby?" I asked.

He didn't answer.

"How could anybody do such a thing?" I couldn't believe it was true.

"There is a power so strong that it could force one to do something against his own will. An evil that can control another being to the point of inflicting illness or committing acts of harm." The words, "You must be careful," trailed from his lips in warning.

It made me wonder how far I could trust any of the people who worked at the trading post. In the end, I knew I could depend on no one but myself.

Losing no time, as soon as I got home, I placed a call to my friend Lisa, who happened to know someone in the higher echelons of the FBI. I was hopeful that through her contact we might be able to get some help. Keeping my fingers crossed, I sat hovered over the phone.

I didn't have long to wait for a response. Whatever she said to her friend, she obviously convinced him, I thought, as I cradled the phone to my ear, listening to the distinguished dry voice.

"I'll see if I can contact the person in charge of crimes on the reservation," he said encouragingly. "I know he can assist you. And, don't worry," he added. "I'm certain I can penetrate the FBI's omnipotent government bureaucracy." I stayed close to the phone and waited for him to make contact with someone to help us.

In a matter of hours, I heard from the Supervisor in charge of Crimes on the Reservation. "The FBI normally doesn't get involved in cases of this type…" he immediately began to inform me.

"Yes, I know. It's not within the FBI's jurisdiction," I finished his sentence under my breath. I could have almost guessed those would be the first words out of his mouth. "That's why I appreciate it all the more," I commended him.

"I want you to know," he continued, his deep voice exuding authority, "that we are assigning this case to our man in Gallup. The agent there is aware of the situation. He has adjusted his schedule accordingly, so that he can meet with you just as soon as possible."

Without further discussion, I quickly jotted the number down on a pad, thanked him, and hung up. I reached for the phone, again.

"Mother!" I said excitedly, listening to her lifeless voice as she answered my call.

"What is it, Sarah? Is there some good news?" she asked. Feeling my enthusiasm, her voice sparked with a glimmer of hope.

"Not as good as I'd like, but I am encouraged. Through a friend's contact with the FBI, we were able to solicit their help. I just spoke with the agent in charge. He would like to meet with us in Gallup, tomorrow, at ten. Can you make it, Mother?"

"Of course I can," she said. "I'll plan to be at your place around four in the morning. Will that give us enough time?"

"I'm sure it will," I answered, feeling Mother's spirits lifting and my thoughts rising with renewed hope.

"I can't tell you, Sarah, how relieved I am, knowing that they have finally agreed to assist in the case."

"I know, Mother. I am too. With their resources, at least now we should make some progress. Besides, the FBI has an image to uphold. They won't be like a bunch of bloodhounds vacuuming the ground with their noses and chasing their tails in circles." Mother's faint laughter cheered me as I hung up the phone.

Meeting us at the door was a young man, perhaps in his late twenties. Not what I had envisioned, I thought. Wearing khaki pants and open-collared, plaid shirt, he didn't have the look of a FBI agent. He identified himself as Special Agent Campbell. My mind raced as I restated the chronology of events. I watched him as he analyzed the information I had given him. His thoughts seemed disconnected. His comments seemed irrelevant.

Surely, he's smart enough to assess the pertinent facts, I thought cynically, raising an eyebrow and briefly linking my eyes with Mother's. Silently, she confirmed my thoughts. Either he was slow-witted, or he was practicing his verbal deception skills. I didn't know which, but I figured I knew why he had been exiled to Gallup.

"I guess it does look a little suspicious," he finally admitted, as we stood to leave.

"Perhaps we were better off with the bloodhounds," I sighed in exasperation. "No wonder they rarely solve any crimes on this reservation," I whispered to Mother, aware that at last count, there had been only one case solved in the past ten years. It was not exactly a record breaking number.

Even though I tried to feel confident that at last a real investigation into the case was underway, my negative opinion had not faded.

CHAPTER IX

When we finally arrived home, I felt like my mind had been put in a blender. It was difficult to solidify my thoughts. Rather than fighting the confusion spinning in my head, I went to bed early.

That night, in the black dark, I heard a faint knock on the door. I stirred, slowly. The knock sounded louder. Wearily, I struggled to open my eyes. Who could it be at this time of night, I wondered? Glancing at the dresser clock, I noticed it was after eleven.

From the hall window, I could see no one.

"Who's there?" I yelled, as I approached the door.

In the dimness, I could see the shadowy figure of a man, his thin frame silhouetted by a street lamp across from my private drive. I watched him as he pulled something from the waistband of his dark blue jeans and shoved it into his jacket pocket. His hand looked waxy in the light. I wish I could see his face, I thought, as I crept by one of the front windows.

"Who is it?" I asked again, still not hearing a reply.

Suddenly, there was a response. "The tile man," a male voice boomed.

"I didn't order any tile, nor would I at this hour. Who are you looking for?"

"Smith," the man said.

"There's nobody here by that name," I called from behind the closed door.

Then, silence.

Through the window, I could see the outline of the man walking beside a red pickup truck. At first, I thought I recognized him. He had a tall lean torso and wore his long, medium brown hair tied back in a ponytail. I remembered seeing a male of a similar description in Cornflower Corners. Lingering suspicions made me think of what Madelyn once told me. "You are dealing with cold blooded killers. They are very dangerous and very violent."

"You are making my life a living hell," I uttered to myself, as I watched him get in his truck and drive away.

For the remainder of the night, I had nightmares. Finally, after falling into a deep sleep just before the early dawn, I was abruptly awakened again.

This time I sat up, alert. Hearing the sound of a fist beating on the door, suddenly my wariness became fear. What's going on, I shuddered, breathing rapidly. Too bad my dog had passed away six months earlier.

"What do you want?" I called out, as I stood by the door.

Nobody answered.

"Who's there?" I called again.

I looked out the window again. But this time, thank God, there was no one there. At least I didn't have to worry about another long sleepless night. It was time to get up.

When I went out to get the newspaper, I glanced at the door to see if anyone had left a note or a business card. Nothing was there.

Clayton's picture had hit every local paper in Northern Arizona. I was hopeful that, by publishing his picture, a member of the public would know something and come forward. Unfolding today's edition of *The Arizona Republic*, I saw his smiling face. Holding his picture to my chest, I pressed it against my heart as if locking it inside would keep him alive.

"Still No Leads in Conway's Disappearance" flashed across the front page. Each day, the headlines were basically the same. I agonized as I read the half-page article.

"It has now been over five weeks…" the first sentence stated. I started to fume. "…since Sinagua Basin resident Clayton Conway disappeared under mysterious circumstances, and investigators are still no closer to solving the case. Conway, 42, was last seen on January 10th at his Blue Sage Trading Post on the Navajo Indian Reservation. Accompanying him was an unidentified male, who was believed to be in his late teens or early twenties.

"Prior to arriving at the trading post, Conway was seen leaving the Coca Cola bottling plant in Chinle, where he was picking up soda for his store. Employees were able to confirm that a white male accompanied him, but were unable to offer a description. There has been no sign of Conway since."

It further stated that "one of Clayton's business associates, who has known him for years, is frustrated with the feeble attempts by the Apache County Sheriff's Office and the other agencies involved in trying to locate Conway. The associate feels that law enforcement agencies are not doing all they could to solve the case…"

Reading on, the words popped out of the paragraph, as paraphrased by the sheriff. "A report has been made by a Payson resident, who claims he spotted Conway's Dodge Diesel on January 12th heading toward Phoenix. However, the time does not jibe with the time the truck was found in Phoenix…" But it did coincide with what Madelyn had said. Then, the dates weren't solid, I thought, apprehensively. This confirmation of her vision sparked new fear.

Were the tenets of her theory correct? Was it, in fact, a contrived conspiracy? For some unknown reason, did the persons responsible believe that I was a threat? Would they really try to kill me? Perhaps I was projecting too much meaning into Madelyn's statement. Had she come to me to discern what I knew? Or was she really trying to protect me? Although impressed with her abilities, the one thing I didn't want to do was to turn prognostications into reality, making it a self-fulfilling prophecy.

Fortunately, daily chores gave my mind something other than fear to focus on. I kept busy for the remainder of the day.

That night, the climate of fear prevailed. It was pervasive. I could almost feel it, like I was being watched. Left to my own resources and defenses, I was glad that earlier in the day I had embraced the opportunity to borrow a gun.

Why? Why don't you come tonight? I silently yelled, looking at the loaded pistol beside my bed. Aroused with a sense of empowerment, anger, and fear, I would have shot to kill.

Weeks went by. The investigation was bogged down as if mired in quicksand. "Leads are still being tracked down…" the newspaper said.

Don't make me laugh, I said silently to myself. Empty talk. That's all it is! I read on.

"Apache County and Navajo Reservation Police are combing the area for any clues that may lead to the whereabouts of Conway. Personnel from the Federal Bureau of Investigation are expected to join the case soon."

The case never seemed to gain momentum, even with all the agencies involved, until one morning when I received a call from Sue in Cornflower Corners. As if by carrier pigeon, she had received some news that there had been a major development in the case. Not knowing what to expect, I held my breath. "Just call Morgan," she said. "Apparently, Kramer's daughter found something, some gruesome evidence, indicating that something bad might have happened. Call right away," she urged.

I dialed the Apache County Sheriff's Office. "John Morgan, please," I said urgently.

"I'm sorry, Deputy Morgan won't be in today. He's somewhere on the reservation," the female voice on the phone volunteered. "There have been some new developments on a case he's working on."

It was true, then. But why hadn't they called me? My trembling fingers fumbled as I dialed the number to the trading post.

"John Morgan, please," I said, stricken with terror at what I might hear.

"He's tied up now and can't come to the phone," the voice replied in rapid annoyance.

"I need to talk with him right now," I demanded, overpowering the voice of the girl who was beginning to object. "This is Sarah, Clayton Conway's sister," I announced.

"Oh, Jesus!" she exclaimed in recognition. Her voice was full of alarm. "You better come up here right away. I found…a knife, a knife," she repeated, "and…blood."

"Bobbie Jo!" I yelled her name. "Please slow down!" Struggling to maintain my composure, I tried to be calm myself.

"This morning, when I was cleaning, I found these things…" she continued, frantically blurting the words, her sentences still disjointed. "Oh! Sarah! It looks like Clayton may have been…murdered."

Unable to speak, I found myself just listening.

"I discovered all these blood-stained rags and towels, including a new towel Clayton bought recently in Phoenix." Her words tumbled out. "There must have been a lot of blood, and a knife…and salt and pepper shakers."

"Wait a minute," I interrupted, fear rising in my throat. "Salt and pepper shakers? Where did you find these things?"

"In the freezer," she said, "And there also was a tablecloth…all wrapped in a plastic bag."

Something didn't ring true. She continued, "It must have happened in the kitchen." My mind struggled to take this all in.

"In which freezer did you discover this evidence?" I asked, trying to determine if those could be the same bloody rags that Clayton stumbled upon last summer. I could still see him holding them up gingerly by his fingertips with a squeamish expression on his face.

"I found them in the big freezer in the wool room," she said. "You know, the one we never use."

"Yes, I know which one," I said, fully aware, thinking surely they must be the same rags. But salt and pepper shakers? A tablecloth…and a brand new bath towel? To my knowledge, they were not in the freezer when we were there. Something did not follow logically.

"Will you put Deputy Morgan on now?" I asked. I waited on the line.

Talking with Morgan, he confirmed that bloody bath towels and the items that Bobbie Jo mentioned had been found. How could he have overlooked a ten-foot long by five-foot deep freezer? I thought skeptically. That's big enough to put a body in! When I asked him why he didn't look inside the freezer during his initial investigation, he simply had no explanation. When I asked why I hadn't been notified of Bobbie Jo's findings, he casually dismissed the question.

"I didn't think it was anything. It was only a small steak knife. The blood could have been from an animal. We used to butcher sheep in there all the time."

I sensed he was hedging. Of one thing I was certain; Clayton hadn't butchered any sheep recently.

Deputy Morgan conceded that, "something might have happened in the kitchen...although it appeared clean when we went over it. Looks like the next step will be to get the crime lab out here to process the scene to see if the blood is human."

When the DPS Crime Lab disclosed their findings of the blood, it hit the papers. I couldn't believe my eyes. I sat staring at the print on the front page of the newspaper, only half-believing it. No! It couldn't be human blood...not Clayton's, anyway, but if not Clayton's, whose blood was it? I was still in a state of denial.

According to the newspaper, after determining that the blood was human, the case had been updated from an "Attempt to Locate" to "Suspected Foul Play." Why don't the investigators keep me apprised of such matters? Why do I always have to find things out in a roundabout manner or from the newspaper? I grumbled, getting more and more irritated at the Apache County Sheriff's Office as I finished reading the short article.

I couldn't help but think that if they had not failed in their search of the property the first time, and had re-classified the case earlier, perhaps

Clayton's truck would not have been stolen the second time while under police surveillance. I believed they had the culprit who possibly stole the vehicle and they let him escape a second time.

Infuriated, I recalled how the Phoenix police had detained a young Hispanic male driving Clayton's truck only ten days after he was reported missing. The male listed his address as "unknown" and his ID didn't come close to matching the information on the registration in the glove box. However, because "their main computer was down" and the vehicle had not yet been listed on the "hot sheet," the truck was not confiscated. Not only was the subject driving it not arrested, but he was allowed to drive the truck away! I wondered how law officers could screw things up so badly.

The "investigation" continued as interviews were conducted with friends, business associates, and possible suspects who might have had some motive. As far as I could see, the police were never going to solve this case.

CHAPTER X

The law enforcement officials who had created endless embarrassment for themselves were now enmeshed in political ridicule, and anxious to restore their reputations. The upcoming year was an election year, and so far, especially during the past two months, they looked like bungling idiots. The lack of communication among the numerous agencies involved was obvious. They were stepping on each other's feet. After the case had been updated to "Suspected Foul Play," Deputy Morgan phoned and asked me to inspect Clayton's residence in Cornflower Corners.

"Be sure to remove the tape from Clayton's message machine and send it to me," John Morgan requested. "We definitely want to know who he'd been talking to."

Oh, fine! Now, I was asked to be Apache County's Deputy Sheriff's Deputy Investigator. My first thought…to ask why he didn't do it himself… was instantly overruled by my second: At least something would get done by somebody.

I quickly agreed, ignoring my uneasy feeling.

The next day, I traveled to Cornflower Corners, and I was surprised to see people in front of the house. They told me that Sue, the lady who leased the bar from Clayton, had taken it upon herself to break in and remove the tape. Upon a quick inspection of Clayton's residence, I noticed his CD player was missing, along with many of his compact discs. Even the antique wagon wheel by the front door was missing. How could anybody take advantage of such a situation? Later, I found out that a vacant house is easy prey for thieves.

After I returned home with the tape from Sue, out of the blue I received a call from Deputy Dawson of Cornflower Corners. That agent insisted that I not send the tape to Deputy Morgan, but instead demanded that I send it to him. I thought, how did he know I had the tape? How did he know Morgan wanted it? What was going on?

This agent stated, "It is my understanding that your brother purchased the Blue Sage Trading Post sometime last summer. Is that correct?"

"Yes. That's correct," I answered. "Clayton was able to negotiate a new lease with the Navajo tribe."

"At the time your brother purchased the trading post, did he know that the previous owner's lease was in arrears and had expired?"

"I'm not sure," I replied, "but I do remember he once said something about 'arrearages' in the neighborhood of $65,000."

"Well," he drawled, with more than a hint of sarcasm, "when he bought this 'money-making' operation, was he aware that the previous owner still owed the tribe a substantial amount of money?"

Where was he going with this? Clayton seldom discussed the details of his business ventures with Mother and me, so the officer's questions puzzled me. Particularly these matters of money and debts. I was getting the impression that the officer knew much more than I about the Blue Sage purchase.

He verified with, "You do know that Sheriff's Deputy Morgan owned the trading post before your brother took it over and that the sheriff himself had owned it before that?" Before I could answer, he added, "See if you can find any paperwork on the transaction with Morgan."

"Surely you don't suspect John Morgan?" I was incredulous.

His reply was a curt, "Just get me the tape and the papers."

I told him I would try to find the information he wanted. And with that, we hung up.

Caught in the cross-fire between the two agencies, plus the thought of Deputy Morgan as a possible suspect, I wasn't certain which way to turn. But as I gathered all the pertinent material in my possession, no matter how innocuous, I decided to bypass both Deputy Dawson and Deputy Morgan.

Having no means of playing the small message micro tape, and without knowing what information it contained, I turned over all my material and the tape to FBI Special Agent Campbell, in order to speed things up in the investigation.

CHAPTER XI

Paranoia had set in. Whom could I trust? My mind was going in circles. And on top of it all, a call from Madelyn brought a new warning. I told her about the several mysterious knocks on my door in the deep of night, adding, "In fact, just last night I awoke to somebody ringing the door bell. This time, the person was claiming to be an airline representative delivering some misplaced luggage."

"That was no coincidence," she replied with absolute certainty and alarm. "My friend, you are in danger! I want you to promise you will not open the door for anyone. Anyone! Do you understand?"

Understand? No. Frightened? She had me convinced. "Okay, Madelyn," I said, "I promise. I will NOT open the door to anyone in the middle of the night." By then she had me leery of everyone, including Madelyn herself, as well as the FBI agent, who blithely dismissed the incidents of the knocks on the door.

She went on to explain some new insights she had gained into the meaning of the vision she had experienced.

"The killing was over property," she said, "...a feud over something to do with property. This was not a crime of opportunity, like a simple break-in and robbery. The robbery was secondary. Also, in my vision, the killers did not act alone. There was at least one other person. Someone who drove a blue pickup truck. I believe the other truck was red."

Red? I remembered the knock on the door and seeing a red pickup truck. Another strange "coincidence?"

I managed to mumble only a weak thank you, as Madelyn ended her call with a superfluous, but well-meant, "Be very careful. Everything tells me you are in real danger."

Meanwhile, Mother and I contributed blood samples for use in a procedure that traces maternally-inherited DNA. The technicians said their analysis would determine if the blood found in the freezer was Clayton's.

Alerted by now to the questionable way most other things were being handled, I objected when I found that John Morgan had been assigned to transport our blood samples to the nearest crime lab in Flagstaff. I wasn't about to have them fall into the wrong hands, especially to someone who may have reason to tamper with evidence.

I asked the FBI to send one of its own personnel in place of Morgan. They refused, but when I persisted in my objections, they finally pressured the sergeant from the Navajo Police to go with him.

A couple of weeks later, I received the DNA report and my world went dark. The tests clearly proved that it was Clayton's blood in the freezer. Sitting on the edge of my bed, I read the confirmation in stunned disbelief. "It can't be Clayton's blood," I tried to convince myself. "It just mustn't be!"

But the impersonal scientific language would not be denied. The blood had been shed by Clayton. And even though the report contained no speculation as to who or what caused the bleeding, I finally admitted to myself that my brother had been viciously attacked, vitally wounded, and possibly killed.

After tossing fitfully all night, I tried to go about my daily routine, but was unable to function effectively. I sat by the window and tried to focus my thoughts. Who could have wanted to kill or even harm my brother? Authorities from three jurisdictions of law enforcement were seeking answers to the same questions, but so far they had no viable suspects other than the "kid" who had been seen with him, and whom they still could neither identify nor find.

Occasionally, as I gazed numbly out the window, I would see someone walking by who looked like Clayton in size and age. My hopes would thrill for an instant before I could force my thoughts back to reality. But even "reality" was open to question. Yes, I had accepted the truth of his assault and wounds, but I clung to the further truth that he was still officially just "missing." Like any other missing person, he could conceivably walk in the door at any time, bandaged, but very much alive. On such frail fabric, I pinned my hopes and tried to stay calm.

My intuition, on the other hand, trusted no such fabric. I "sensed" that finding him would bring no comfort. Thus torn, I remained braced for the news.

The phone rang. The Supervisor in Charge of Crimes on the Reservations said, "I need to meet with you in person." His deep masculine voice awkwardly conveyed that familiar "bad news" tone that's really saying, "I don't know how to tell you this, but…"

"Wait a minute," I interrupted. "Since your office is based in Phoenix, could you come over to my house so we could discuss this in person?"

I slowly hung up and thought for a minute before calling Mother. I decided it was better she hear the news directly from the source, rather than my interpretation later.

As soon as I heard her voice on the phone, I said, "Please come over. The Navajo Supervisor of Crimes is coming with news of Clayton."

"I'll be there quickly," she said.

I stood in nervous idleness as I waited for her and for the man who would tell us what I already dreaded.

Mother arrived first. I tried to find words to prepare her, but the doorbell rang before I had a chance.

At the doorway, I searched his face, silently pleading for a sign that my fears were groundless, that my intuition was wrong. Nothing.

I asked him to join us in the living room. Obviously uncomfortable, he removed his "Supervisor" cap, came in and stood silently, twisting his cap and groping for opening words. Quietly, I took him off the hook.

"You've found him, haven't you?" The husky whisper was firm, but barely audible.

He nodded "Yes." His head still bent in silence told me what he didn't want to say. My brother was dead.

"Are you positive it's Clayton?" My voice quivered with emotion, no longer able to hide the anguish. "Please, tell us it isn't true," I cried, tears streaming down my cheeks.

"I'm sorry," he said.

Unsteadily, I sat down and embraced Mother. I had been trying to prepare us for this dreadful moment, but even the merciful veil of numbness that had enshrouded me could not protect me from the terrifying truth.

Having found his voice, the supervisor went on to explain who had accidentally found Clayton's body. The "who" was surprising and the "how" was maddening, but as he described "where," I shriveled in horror.

When he left, I was still in shock, but I instinctively turned to comfort Mother. Her glazed eyes betrayed her merciful retreat into some unreachable and alien place. I could offer her no peace.

I steeled myself to make two dreaded phone calls to my sons and prepare for my brother's funeral the following week.

CHAPTER XII

Rain was beating against the roof. The hands on the clock crept toward five o'clock as I lay awake, devastated by depression. Having surrendered myself to the same recurring nightmare, I had dreamed of the hooded forms cloaked in black. Again, their evil faces were masked in distortions of depravity. Despising the world, I was dying spiritually, emotionally, and mentally, embroiled in an inferno of hatred.

From the kitchen window, I could see the rain falling in quarter size drops. Why? Why did it have to pour today, the day of Clayton's funeral, I brooded. While crouching over the kitchen counter, propping myself on my elbows, I stared at the inky sky.

The rain flirted with the Valley all morning, falling like teardrops upon the windowpane. Perhaps this is just God's way of expressing sorrow, I thought, as I continued to stare at the black clouds through the open shutters. Mesmerized, I watched them churn violently overhead.

Making the same swirling motion with my coffee, I stirred the sludgy-looking remains. It was my ninth cup, and by now it looked like motor oil. Tipping my cup up, I took the last gulp.

Impatiently, I waited until ten o'clock before placing my call.

"Hi, Sue. What are the weather conditions up there?" I inquired hesitantly, knowing that Cornflower Corners was expected to have another two inches of overnight rainfall.

"Oh, Sarah," she said, dismayed. "It's been raining cats and dogs. We've had three consecutive days of rain with no sign of let up. I'm so glad that you called. The minister wants to know if we should hold the service in the gymnasium, as we alternately planned, or do you want to face off the fury of nature?"

"Let's wait a little longer before making a decision," I suggested, thinking Clayton would have liked an open-air service, since he preferred a religion inspired by nature with no confining walls. His beliefs were like many Native Americans, I reflected, since their place of worship was their ancestral land. Although he wasn't a native, surely Clayton deserved to have his ceremony performed in that peaceful cemetery with its sacred beauty.

It is all a part of *hozho*, I thought, recalling the Navajo word for beauty. Beauty is not only the grass, the plants and the flowers; it is also the raincloud formations and thunderheads.

I told Sue to proceed with the original plans unless she heard otherwise. Having made the decision, I hung up. I was sure Clayton would rather have been buried on the reservation. Like the Navajos, he was tied to the land by ancient sacred cords. But, in light of the nature of the tragedy, I decided it would be best to have him interred in Cornflower Corners. I wasn't about to upset the natural order of the Indian world.

Standing before the bathroom mirror, I grappled with the buttons on my blouse. After dressing, I stood still, feeling a sudden wince of pain. My brother was in the prime of life, less than one month shy of his forty-third birthday. He was so young to have his life extinguished. The tears rolled down my gaunt face. Surely these eyes don't belong to me. I shuddered as I saw the tears streaming down the deep furrows that weren't there a few months ago. As I turned away in disgust, my son timidly poked his head through the open door. "Grandma is here," Preston said solemnly.

Moving at a lethargic pace, I met Mother in the hall. She looked small and drawn, like a shadow of her former self.

Several of my closest friends had offered to drive. However, today I preferred to be alone with my family as the four of us silently drove to the tiny principality cradled by purple mountains.

As if by divine intervention, the pale yellow sun had poked through the clouds. By the time we arrived, it was beaming. Squinting at the bursting rays of light fanning out between the white puffy clouds, I smiled with my eyes. The site was perfect for the evocation of grief, a truly hallowed ground.

Although not in bloom, wild irises bordered the gravesites marking the final resting-places of generations who had lived and died in this rugged land. It was so beautiful and immaculately maintained, I thought, looking at the wooden crosses and ancient-looking tombstones. It had such quaintness…an old-fashioned charm. Yet it all seemed so surreal…having the intense irrationality of a dream, I thought as I looked at the closed casket, draped with garlands of flowers. Trying to maintain my emotional equilibrium, I walked with Mother to the gate. Outside the fence, a stray dog sniffed the residual moisture in the air. Only in a place like this would a dog be attending a funeral. I muffled a half-hearted sigh.

Reaching down to stroke the matted fur on the dog's back, I looked into his mournful eyes. "You look sad, too, but probably for other reasons," I smiled, reflecting on how Native Americans refer to all animals as "brothers and sisters." It reminded me of how they view the value of life. They believe that they are a part of a delicately balanced world, in which all forms of life are interrelated and that only man can upset that balance. As a people, the Diné have a fundamental respect for life.

I looked at the somber-faced crowd, watching as colleagues and friends of Clayton's hugged each other and wiped tears from their eyes. The people who live here are a different breed, I observed, as a callused hand clutched mine.

"I'm so sorry, Ma'am," he said sorrowfully. "We'll all miss him."

My thoughts followed him as he walked away with his cowboy hat tipped forward.

Blessed with the people who have kept its rural character, this sleepy town cared about its residents. Everybody knew everybody here. As I looked into the distance at the murky, encroaching waters of Sinagua Creek, threatening to cut a new channel, I was reminded that in a crisis the town's residents all pitched in to help each other. Lingering floodwaters made worse by overnight rains were wreaking havoc on this tiny, rustic community. By now, the creek was bisected into two halves as floodwaters spilled over acres, closing the only land bridge across the usually dry creek.

I was overwhelmed with the outpouring of love and condolences. Even those people living on the eastern bank had refused to heed earlier evacuation warnings and were seemingly more concerned with getting to the funeral than with their own welfare. Smiling inwardly, I thought about the massive community effort involved. In order for all to attend the services, the town's residents ferried those who were stranded on a make-shift six-wheel vehicle referred to as the "Creek Crosser." With my city girl's eyes focused back on the crowd, I observed the tattered and muddy boots and marveled at their pioneering spirit.

We were all seated around the copper-colored casket. There was a short reflective silence before the minister began to speak. "Some people come into our lives and quickly go. Others stay for a while and leave footprints on our hearts, and we're never the same." Ironically, it was the same verse that was printed on a card that I later found among my brother's belongings. I cried softly. Hearing Mother's faint sobs, I dabbed my eyes. Feeling her pain, I sat in stoic dignity.

I listened as one of the town's most prominent citizens delivered the eulogy. "Clayton always yearned for a rural lifestyle, following his passion in pursuit of the American dream," he said in words charged with emotion. As he spoke, questions mulled in my mind. How many untold numbers of dreams would be forever buried? What is the price of forsaken dreams? I questioned. My life hasn't always been easy; nonetheless, I have been blessed with two wonderful sons who mean the world to me, as well as enjoyable times with Mother and my friends. Life's lessons sometimes teach us to re-evaluate our priorities.

"Clayton blessed us with his memory," the speaker said, bowing his head in conclusion. "May he rest in peace."

Seeing the sun's rays bounce off the jagged peaks, turning them the color of honey, I remembered Camille's words: "All things are alive, even the rocks."

Longingly, I looked at my brother's casket, noticing it was the same bronze shade as the mountains that surrounded it. I thanked God for allowing Clayton to be my brother, my children's uncle, and my mother's son, who played an intricate role in our lives. Silently, I prayed. "May he 'be' in peace." Seated together with my family, we listened as the minister blessed the site. Squeezing each other's hands in silent support, we rose. After saying my final farewell and placing the last rose gently on top of Clayton's coffin, I watched as they lowered it into the ground.

A soft breeze rippled through the somber congregation, stirring my thoughts. "Dear God, help us bear our burdens and ease our hurts," I prayed, taking a wadded clump of tissue from my purse. I was glad this was over, glad to feel my sons' embraces. As they escorted Mother, who walked with courage to the car, I took a final glimpse at the gentle rolling hills where Clayton was laid to rest. He belonged here in a place where the songs of countless birds melded harmoniously with the silent grandeur of the terrain. Every flower, every bush, every tree seemed to unite with the human spirit in preparation for the soul's journey to Eternal Life.

A peaceful calm fell over me. Knowing that Clayton was spiritually at peace with his Maker, I closed the gate.

And the rain resumed.

CHAPTER XIII

A few days after the funeral, I met with Special Agent Campbell, who informed me that, "Now, it's murder!" The case had been upgraded from Suspected Foul Play to Homicide. Clayton had been found in one of the outbuildings, only ten feet from the main door of the trading post. According to the autopsy report, he had been shot in the back of the head at point blank range, the .22 caliber bullet entering at the base of the skull. Gruesome pictures verified the result.

His remains were well preserved, especially considering the length of time. It had been almost three months, but nobody had looked inside that building during the entire time. Why? Because it was locked! Their answer was really that stupidly simple. It would have been laughable under other circumstances. It didn't make sense. But, it didn't make sense that they had originally overlooked the freezer, either.

Worse yet, we found that Deputy Morgan had never turned over much of the evidence to the crime lab. All those pop and beer cans…I was certain that they contained somebody's fingerprints and DNA, but now we would never know. According to the FBI, the evidence had been left in the back of Morgan's open pickup truck for months, so all traces of fingerprints and DNA would have been erased by the wind, rain, and snow. Why? Because he didn't know how to categorize it! That was his explanation. I didn't buy that. He was too smart. Either he was criminally lazy or he was covering up something.

There were so many suspicious facts. Why did it take Kramer, that snake who always toted the gun, one full day to get in touch with me after Clayton's truck was first discovered abandoned? Furthermore, why hadn't he been at the trading post on Monday to meet with Clayton? After all, that was the scheduled date for him to officially take over the operation, but he was hundreds of miles from there. Did he know Clayton wouldn't be there?

Did somebody know it was to be Clayton's last weekend and plan accordingly, thinking it was now or never? Sadly, I realized that Clayton might be alive today if he had not gone to the trading post that final weekend.

Regretfully, I was never able to see Clayton's body. By the time I was notified, his body was already en route to the FBI Forensic Headquarters in New Mexico, where they performed the autopsy. It was Clayton, they assured me, confirming that his identity had been positively established through fingerprints. I was even skeptical of that, recalling how all the experts had also assured me they had searched the property thoroughly. To think he was right there, right under their eyes, not more than ten yards from the windmill...

The same windmill that was in my vision and stood next to the deep hole. The same deep hole that Madelyn had seen in her vision, its murky depths filled with water and spiders. The same place that Madelyn had described in chilling detail, as being "nearby" when she demonstrated her psychic ability to the various law enforcement agencies. The FBI, jealously guarding their reputation and looking askance at "unscientific" things, had refused any psychic assistance. Yet, I am convinced that if they had not resisted the notion, they might have found his body sooner...a body that had been wrapped in a tarpaulin of sorts and dumped into a well, housed in an abandoned shed.

Disgusting as it was, it finally came down to two things in the end; my brother was dead, and there was nothing I could do to change that. However, I was tormented by the memories of "seeing" the last moment of his life.

Perhaps, there was something I could have done to save him. I cried, suffering the intolerable pangs of regret.

After my visit with Agent Campbell, I had so many unanswered questions. I felt drawn to visit the trading post to see once again the actual site where the events took place.

CHAPTER XIV

It was early morning. The cold mist hanging over the trading post was more fog than rain. No light was visible through the trees screening the compound on my right, as I drove along the deserted road leading up to the trading post.

Suddenly, a dark shadow swooped low, with a startling whir of wings, to pounce on some small creature scurrying across the road. My hands gripped the wheel. I turned it sharply to the left as the Great Horned Owl lifted its wings and was gone with its prey. What a creepy place! There was no sign of my earlier fascination with the isolated area.

As I got out of my car, I saw that Kramer was standing against the open doorway. "I'm glad you could come," he sneered.

"I bet you are," I sneered back.

Shortly before his death, Clayton had entered into an agreement with Jerome Kramer that allowed him to purchase a portion of the trading post. The agreement included a stipulation that he would manage the trading post and take care of daily operations, thus freeing up Clayton's time.

"I took over this office," Kramer said, "immediately after Clayton's body was found. I would have preferred to wait, but I wanted to make sure his employees did not remove any of his papers out of a misguided sense of loyalty."

"Are the files all there?" I asked.

"No. I mailed the current files to my wife in Cornflower Corners this morning. She does all of my bookwork. She should be receiving them tomorrow."

"You did what?" I was very upset. "You should have consulted me before doing that."

"If you really want them, I'll arrange to have my wife meet you at the Cornflower Post Office after she gets off work tomorrow. Agreed?"

I reluctantly shook his hand. Remembering what Morgan had told me about counting my fingers, I found myself checking them.

My feet moved of their own volition toward the small weathered building next to the windmill. "This is it? Isn't it?"

"Yeah, he was there all the time!"

I could go no farther. Suddenly, I had a strong urge to leave this place. The sense of sadness here was overwhelming.

I got in the car and drove home while sobbing. I asked out loud in a pleading voice, "Why did my brother have to die the way he did? He didn't deserve this. His death was painful, ugly, and unnatural." I managed to pull myself together before reaching the Phoenix city limits.

When I got home, Mother was in her favorite chair. "What did you find out, Sarah?" she asked.

"Not much, only that Kramer sent the current files to his wife. Hopefully, I can intercept her tomorrow before she has a chance to go through them and dispose of anything." I was certain there had to be some clues in those files.

"What about the key?" Mother asked.

"Oh, drat! I forgot to ask Kramer." Even something simple like by whom and how Clayton was found is vague. There were three conflicting explanations as to how Camille's cousins, who had been re-hired after Clayton had fired them, stumbled upon the body. The one consistent factor, though, was the issue of the key that Lenny claimed was hanging on the wall by the inside door where it had always been. Yet, prior to that, nobody seemed to be able to find it, at least not during the initial investigation.

Mother kept prying. I told her, "I don't want to talk about all that today. It's a dead end; rehashing what we already know won't help. If we don't get our hands on those files, we're never going to find out who murdered Clayton."

The next afternoon, as planned, I drove to the Cornflower Post Office, arriving at 4:00 p.m., but there was no sign of Mrs. Kramer. Don't tell me she's not going to show up, I thought. Just then, a light blue pickup truck pulled into the lot.

"I'm late," the woman yelled out of her truck window. Mrs. Kramer was about forty-five, although it was hard to tell her age: blonde hair slightly gray, brown eyes behind silver-rimmed glasses, a little above average in height, a little below average in weight; the kind of woman who, if the police asked you, you would very accurately describe as average.

We walked over to the panel of post office boxes and opened her box. It was empty.

"Oh, well," she shrugged. "Maybe the package will be here tomorrow. I'll forward the files to you."

After she left, I asked the postmaster if Mrs. Kramer had received any overnight mail.

"Yes," he said, "a large package from her husband."

"Why wasn't the package in her box?"

"It was. She has two Post Office boxes."

I take back what I said about Mrs. Kramer. She's not average. She's smarter than I thought.

It was a month later and we still weren't any closer to knowing the truth about what happened to my brother.

That night, my psychic friend Madelyn stopped by. "This waiting is frustrating," she said. "You'd think the police would have produced some leads by now. I'm going up to the trading post tomorrow; I'll find some answers."

Bitterly affected by the tragedy, Madelyn set out at first light for the trading post, determined to uncover evidence that would lead her to a suspect. She had suggested that I go with her. But the last thing I wanted to do was to be up there, in that remote place guarded by a dozen or so miles of unpaved twisting road, with Clayton's business partner, Kramer, Deputy Morgan…or even Madelyn for that matter.

Content to stay at home, I waited her return from a day that lasted well over fourteen hours. Forcing myself to stop hyperventilating long enough to manage a smile, I was immensely relieved to see her truck pull into the drive.

"You won't believe it," she said, bolting through the open door. "Kramer is painting the entire crime scene area and has John Morgan's permission!" she continued, with shocked misgivings. "If any evidence has been overlooked, which is more than a likely possibility, you better believe it's been destroyed now." Angrily, she gave me the details:

"If I had had my way, I might have gotten some answers. But, no! I had no sooner arrived at the post than Deputy Morgan intercepted me in the hall. He certainly acted odd, almost like he was jittery with my being there." She continued to tell me how he had latched onto her arm and refused to let her out of his grasp. He deliberately attempted to steer her away from anything that looked remotely suspicious, and instead tried to turn her in the direction of his own theory, which was "simple robbery." He stated it as if he had a corner on the truth. Since he scoffed at her version of the crime scenario, she ignored his simplistic denouncement.

"From my perspective," she grumbled, "it was a total waste of time. I bet I didn't spend five minutes there, including the time I spent with Morgan when he escorted me through that rambling, old trading post."

In summing up her trip, although deeming it a disaster, one thing had been revealed to her, and that was the need for me to observe first hand what was going on up there and to "take charge."

If I had had a clue that evidence was not being protected, perhaps I could have intervened. Now the question was, what should I do? Should

I stay in Phoenix and continue to try to resolve all the urgent legal and business problems associated with the probate, or should I drop everything and tackle the crime situation at the trading post?

CHAPTER XV

It was a balancing act, I realized, sometimes wishing that fate hadn't entwined me in this mess. Clayton had so many properties I needed to contend with. The critical factor was having enough money to resolve the issues. Therein lay the problem.

Financially, Clayton was just beginning to see his way clear. He had barely completed his arrangement with his new business partner, Jerome Kramer. Although he believed he was reasonable in his expectations when he sold Kramer a fifty percent interest in the trading post, and thought he had held out for what he considered a fair deal, the contract he negotiated was a very complicated transaction.

Clayton supposedly received a large amount of cash from this transaction. I assumed it was in Clayton's newly installed safe at the trading post that I was waiting for the FBI to open. To make matters worse, I found out that Clayton had entered into a separate agreement, which eventually became part of the contract, and that required him to pay a large lump sum of money on a specified date to satisfy a loan on another of his properties. Kramer held that note. The language of the agreement was structured so as to leave Clayton few options. Under the terms and conditions of the agreement, Clayton had waived his rights in the event of a foreclosure, foregoing the ability to seek relief from the courts. The transaction was designed in such a manner that all of his property in Cornflower Corners would automatically revert back to Jerome Kramer, the prior owner, if that balloon payment was even one minute late. All in all, the very nature of the transaction held open the possibility that Clayton had been manipulated. A far more serious question now cried out for an answer: Had he been set up?

Why Clayton had agreed to such conditions baffled me. Perhaps he was too trusting, or perhaps he was desperate…like I was now, knowing that if I was unable to raise the money, I stood to lose the family's entire investment in Cornflower Corners, which included the saloon and steakhouse, a commercial building and Laundromat, an RV park, boat storage facilities, and approximately thirteen acres of prime land. All of which had substantial equity.

As doomsday neared, with the financial burden now shifted to me, I approached Jerome Kramer and asked for an extension, which he verbally granted. I believed him, and why not? He appeared to be honorable. However, when it came to putting it in writing, he stalled. Then, from out of nowhere, he pulled the rug out from under me, leaving me with less than a month to raise the money. After that stunt, Kramer and I didn't exactly have a warm personal rapport. However, I refused to be cowed. It only served to amplify my efforts. Although not eager to confront Kramer again, I opted to go to the trading post anyway, and "take charge" as Madelyn had urged.

Now, who could I entice to go with me? I wasn't going up there alone again.

Lisa was one of those dear friends I only see every once in awhile, usually at social functions—the same friend who was instrumental in getting the FBI involved in the case. Whenever we met, we vowed to see more of each other and to act on some of the great adventures that the two of us always imagined. She would be willing to go, I thought, as I coaxed her.

"Please, Lisa," I urged. "It would mean so much to me. Besides, you've never seen my brother's trading post."

"Sure, Sarah," she said, after a long pause. "I'm always game for an adventure." It didn't take much convincing. We left early the next morning.

Not knowing what to expect once we arrived at the trading post, I had brought a gun along, but was afraid to tell Lisa, not wanting her to misconstrue it as an implied threat of danger. As we talked, I was startled to learn that she had brought one also. Although we laughed upon the discovery, we knew the element of danger was real.

"Who do you think wanted to see your brother dead?" Lisa asked.

"If I knew that, I'd know who killed him. I believe it was Kramer. Yet, I don't trust Deputy Morgan, especially with any evidence.

"What little evidence he did preserve," I added, "turned out to be dog hairs."

"I read once," Lisa said, "where you can transfer fingerprints with some kind of sticky tape."

"Without leaving a trace? Maybe an expert could, but not an amateur. Besides, there's no way Morgan would be able to do that. You should have seen the way he dusted for fingerprints."

"You don't know."

"I know the murder is connected to Clayton's business."

"Know from evidence or know from intuition?"

"Just know," I said, without revealing it was the psychic who told me.

I used to think danger was abstract...something that happened to somebody else. That no longer was the case. I was aware now that crime doesn't recognize classes. Impersonal, without reference or connection, it touches at random.

I also realized I was flirting with danger, especially now that there was an unknown killer on the loose. I was not quite sure that I wasn't being set up to become his next victim, targeted for murder. Thinking of what Madelyn had said, I remembered the time when Morgan had made some sort of an excuse to leave the room at my house. Like Madelyn, he too was gone for a long time. What was he doing when he locked himself in my bathroom that first day when he visited my house? Could he have been putting poisonous pills in my Excedrin bottles so that he could get rid of me? She had also said, "Someone might attempt to interject themselves into the case." I trembled inwardly with the sobering realization that the person she was talking about could even be her. Enough, Sarah! I said to myself. At the rate you're going, you'll be casting a suspicious eye on the Pope!

"It shouldn't be much longer," I said, directing my attention back to Lisa, who was busy taking pictures through the open window of the car. She seemed in no hurry, I thought, as I watched her poking her head out the window, looking at the anvil-shaped clouds.

"This turned out to be such a beautiful day," I sighed, as I reached over for a snack that Lisa had tucked in our lunch basket. While I nibbled on cheese and crackers, I told her about life on the reservation.

"On the 'Rez', as Clayton called it, lie some of the most unique and rugged landscapes in the world. This sacred plot of earth is home to both the Navajo and Hopi nations. There's a conflict between the two tribes that arose mostly over land. The federal government attempted to settle it back in the late 1800s, but that only seemed to cause more contention. This Navajo-Hopi land dispute, having deep cultural roots, is still not fully settled. Even so, Lisa, I hardly think we'll need to duck from flying arrows," I joked, as she responded by quickly drawing her head in from the window.

"On Navajo land, you'll find there's a lot of activity. There is even a little shopping center in Pinon. However, for the most part, it's quiet isolation. You feel like you've left one reality and entered another. In this setting of vivid colors and sun and shadows, it's hard to imagine the blood and death that occurred here.

"Sorry, I didn't mean to get off on a tangent." I continued... "It's like stepping back one hundred years in time, especially when you cross over into Hopi land, which is divided from the rest of the Navajo reservation by an invisible line formed in the shape of a rectangle.

"Right smack in the middle of this Indian country sits Black Mesa, a massive mound shaped in the form of a gnarled hand. Although starting as a huge escarpment, this formation eventually dwindles to a series of thick, deformed fingers jutting out, named First, Second, and Third Mesa, and separated by dry washes. Hopi tribal members reside in tiny secluded villages on these mesas.

"Hopefully, we will get to see at least a portion of that today," I said, as we continued to chat along the way.

There must be some significance in the number "four" in the Navajo culture, I decided, after Lisa mentioned something pertaining to the "Four Corners area." This term, refers to the place where the corners of four states (Arizona, Colorado, New Mexico, and Utah) meet at a contiguous point on a northeast segment of the Navajo Nation.

"It must be their lucky number," I mused, thinking of the four sacred mountains of emergence, four sacred stones, and four crops. Lisa had reminded me that the Four Corners area has frequently served as a backdrop for epic Hollywood Westerns.

"The Four Corners area is an amazing place," I said, while we continued in that general direction. "You needn't worry, Lisa," I smiled. "I can guarantee, you'll use up plenty of film where we're going today."

Kramer happened to be standing outside the trading post as we came to a stop. Walking over to the car as I got out, he held out his hand. His polite smile did not deceive me. Ignoring him, opting not to engage in an awkward handshake, I continued to walk at a brisk pace to the door.

"Too good to shake hands," he muttered, following me with his eyes.

Obviously, Kramer hadn't changed a bit. He was just as repulsive as ever. Why Clayton chose him for a business partner was beyond me.

Lisa, who had been looking the other way the entire time, turned to face us. Sensing just how nasty and personal this battle of wills had become, she made a valiant effort to distract us.

"This is some road," she commented, referring to the twisting cobra-hooded spiral.

"Sure is. It's enough to keep most visitors away," Kramer said. "And, of the few who do make it up here, some end up dead." He displayed a contemptuous grin.

Whether that was a veiled threat to force me to leave, or perhaps, an unintentional slip of the tongue, the remark did not go unnoticed by Lisa. She rolled her eyes in my direction.

"It's little wonder you don't get along with him," she whispered, her eyes catching mine.

I decided to ignore the threatening context of Kramer's last statement. "I would like to go over the key points of the tragedy with you, if you don't mind."

"What would you like to know?"

"First off, I would like to know why you had Clayton sign that agreement on the Cornflower Corners property. Was it your intention to foreclose on Clayton from the start? From what I've heard, you couldn't wait to have him out of the way." I stared hard at Kramer, forcing my gaze not to waver.

"That was between your brother and me. Now, what I want to know is, do you have the money?"

"I am not here to discuss that now," I said, thinking…it's always wise to be careful when confronting a snake.

"Well, you've got less than a month to come up with it," he reminded me. "And then C.C. will be mine."

"The hell it will," I said recklessly, swallowing the words "over my dead body." My comment only seemed to rile him more as we engaged in a brief but pointed verbal exchange. It was his turn to speak and he didn't miss a beat.

"I'm going to own that place," he repeated. "You wait and see. Don't think of it as a threat," he hissed, "it's more of a commitment."

"I don't suppose you remember telling me I had a thirty day extension?"

Throwing his head back, he laughed. It was then that I first noticed a conspicuous scar on his throat. It almost looked as if it had penetrated the carotid artery. Maybe I wasn't the only one who detested this man, I thought, hearing his venomous laugh as I turned and walked out the door.

"Well, so much for that discussion," I said to Lisa in resignation.

"Which I notice got pretty heated!"

"By the way, Lisa, what exactly were you reaching for in your purse?"

"I wasn't reaching for my gun, if that's what you mean. Honest." She smiled that irrepressible smile.

If nothing else, at least I don't think Kramer will be doing any more remodeling, especially at my expense, I thought, reveling in the expression on his face when I handed him the legal letter from my attorney. As I walked out the door, I saw the freshly painted walls and the paintbrushes and buckets stacked in the kitchen. He wouldn't be tampering with more evidence, either, I thought with satisfaction. But I was wrong.

We had no sooner gotten home than I received a call. It was from an FBI agent in Gallup.

"I'm sorry," he began, explaining that he had to change our previously scheduled appointment. We were to meet with Kramer at the trading post to open the new floor safe that Clayton had installed prior to his disappearance.

I was furious. "Wouldn't you know, the one thing that I was counting on you to do. You've certainly had ample time. I've waited over a month for you to open it. Now it'll probably be months before you get around to it," I railed.

"...I was unable to reach you," the agent said patiently, "so I called Jerome Kramer to see if we could re-schedule for later in the month. It looks like we won't need to go up there after all. It's my understanding that Kramer already hired a locksmith to open it." He was seemingly unconcerned.

"He what?" I couldn't believe my ears. Outrage followed outrage, yet the FBI wasn't concerned. Why? Why don't they care? "That belonged to Clayton!" I said. "There could have been money inside or even some incriminating evidence. Something that could have possibly led us to a suspect. Who knows what was in that safe!" I was purple with rage.

"Kramer does," the agent said, "and he said it was empty."

"Oh, sure. I'm certain that Clayton went to all the trouble and expense to have it installed just to put 'nothing' in it. How does Kramer get away with doing something like this?" I shouted. "If I broke into someone's safe and flouted the law like that, I'd be in jail."

"I know," he said sympathetically, "but there's nothing we can do."

"Why not? I suppose that's not your jurisdiction either," I raged.

His answer was vague as he mumbled the same nothing that I had become accustomed to hearing.

Weeks went by as I commuted from my job at the insurance agency in the Valley and tackled the mess that littered Clayton's desk in Cornflower Corners. Each day, I pored over material and gained new insights as I attempted to resolve the legal and financial problems associated with his numerous businesses.

Luck, for some reason, was with me—or my prayers were answered. When the balloon payment came due on the Cornflower Corners properties, much to Kramer's dismay, I managed to obtain the money by re-financing another property.

Officially, I had been appointed Receiver of Clayton's estate and this allowed me a great deal of flexibility. However, in order to comply with the probate requirements, I had been forced to make decisions that I normally wouldn't make, like allowing the insurance on the properties to lapse, so that all other existing debts could be paid. These matters kept bothering me as I went to bed each night.

I began dreaming.

At first, I heard screaming sirens. Then I saw huge orange plumes and thick billowing smoke. Something was burning at full intensity, but what? Firefighters were on the scene, trying to extinguish the flames. Then, gray smoke blocked out the moon and stars, and ashes drifted slowly from the skies. I awoke, perspiring. Suddenly, a warning clicked in my brain.

There was going to be a fire and I had no insurance. Could it be true? Was there really going to be a fire? Or was I becoming the victim of my own imagination? Panic-stricken, I arranged for insurance coverage on the properties. Unfortunately, I did not completely trust my instincts and limited it to less than a third of the properties' values. I couldn't truly believe that a fire would occur.

Then it happened, not more than two weeks later.

"Brace yourself, Sarah," Sue said, when I answered the phone.

It was five o'clock in the morning, so I knew this was not a social call.

"What now?" I responded, poised to be brave about any catastrophe that might possibly have occurred.

"I wish I didn't have to tell you this," she said, "but last night there was a fire, a blazing fire, and the Cornflower Corners Store and Steakhouse burned to the ground."

I was sick to my stomach. Just once, I wished I could hear some good news, I thought, but I knew at this point that whatever she had to say couldn't be worse than what had already happened. It was like having a bad dream that never ends. All the questions I asked her about the fire were only answered by more questions, the same two that never were resolved. Who and why?

The next day, grounded in reality, I stood before the ashes, smelling the acrid smoke. I was convinced more than ever of the reality of curses as I pictured the *Chindi* carrying their dark-hooded forces with them, invulnerable to any human acts of retaliation. Once again, the image of the faceless spirits, devoid of almost everything except shape, slid into my mind like a writhing, slithering serpent. As the black, hollow figures looked down into the abyss, their gaping mouths opened into a poisonous, perverted laugh. Were they responsible for my brother's murder? Did they start the fire? What other secrets did they conceal within their hooded forms?

If the *Chindi* represents evil, did Kramer have a pact with the devil?

"Why didn't those evildoers stay up at the trading post?" I said in a voice loud enough to be heard by the fire investigator, who was standing beside me. "Haven't they already done enough to my family and me?" I raised my voice in frustration.

He looked at me as if I was crazy, even more so after I attempted to give him a brief run-down on the *Chindi*. "If you ever hear the *Chindi*, you will never forget the sound. It's eerie, really eerie."

"I understand how you feel," he humored me, "and I somewhat agree with you. Based on conversations that I've had with a number of the area's residents about your brother's murder, I believe what happened here could very well have had something to do with revenge. Even so, Mrs. Simms, I hardly think we can consider a spirit a suspect."

"I know. It's just that nobody is ever held accountable for his or her actions around here. This is just one more example among many. It's heartbreaking. I feel like this can't be happening to me," I said, my tears invoking his sympathy.

"I'm sure it's extremely frustrating," the Fire Marshall said in an effort to console me, "and some things just don't add up," he agreed.

"You're telling me," I blurted. "You'd have to be deaf, dumb, and blind to think this wasn't arson. Even the old timers in Cornflower Corners know this place was torched. It's pretty obvious. Why else would the hose that had been by the back door for the last fifteen years have been removed?"

"I must admit, the fire appeared suspicious right from the start. It looks like it began in the area next to the kitchen. Then it spread hot and fast, like it had been fueled, so fast, in fact, that the local fire department right next door was unable to extinguish the flames. Some things are beyond our control," he went on, trying to placate me. "Now, going back to the investigation, Mrs. Simms, the truth of the matter is that I suspect, but can't prove, that this fire was deliberately set. Therefore, I have no choice but to rule it a fire of undetermined origin."

"Oh, I bet that blankety-blank so and so, Jerome Kramer is gloating over this right now," I said, consigning him to hell.

"Do you think Kramer started the fire?"

"I don't know. But I do know that he was visibly upset when I paid off the loan on this property. I'm sure he was banking on his belief that Clayton wouldn't be able to come up with the money, especially with all of his other debts. Kramer had been fairly certain that I wouldn't be able to satisfy the loan. In the agreement Kramer had with my brother, Cornflower Corners would have been easy pickin's."

The Fire Marshall looked doubtful, though he humored me with his silence.

But I knew that Kramer wanted the Cornflower Corners Store more than anything. If he couldn't have it, no one would.

Among the bleak ironies, I could never say that I didn't dream it would happen. Because, I did!

It was hard to sustain order in my life. Even though I reduced my scope by taking only one day at a time, I was still unprepared for Clayton's absence, not only in terms of grief, but also in business. All kinds of matters had either been overlooked or neglected, including two IRS liens. Since Clayton had a degree in law and in business, I felt he must have been dealing with too many issues and not taking proper care of his businesses. In that respect, interspersed among other things, was a liquor license he forgot to renew. "There goes $45,000," I muttered, as I tossed it in the pending folder.

The businesses continued to require most of my attention as I resolved what seemed to be an endless series of problems. Sadly, there was no way we could afford to replace the old Cornflower Corners Store and Steakhouse, but even if we could, I knew the memory would never be the same. One thing did boomerang in my favor. Out of the insurance proceeds, we were at least able to pay off the existing debt.

The phone interrupted my thoughts as it rang. I rushed to the kitchen to answer it.

"Hello," I said between breaths as the voice began to speak without introduction.

"Do you have a minute Sarah?" the girl asked.

"Bobbie Jo. Is that you? I thought I recognized your voice. That's weird you should call. I was just thinking about you. What's up?" I was half-afraid to ask, although I wasn't as apprehensive about Bobbie Jo as I was about her father.

"There are a couple of things I must tell you that I think you'll find shocking," she began.

"Yesterday, when I was cleaning, I found a bullet lodged in the wall in the kitchen. I don't know if it has anything to do with Clayton's murder or not, but I can assure you that we didn't put the slug in the wall," she said, quickly absolving herself and her father of any wrongdoing. Her observation eclipsed all other absurdities. It was unfathomable that no one had noticed this earlier.

"There was also a shell casing over in the corner on the floor. I can't imagine how we missed seeing that stuff," she said, embarrassed. "At any rate, Morgan is coming over today to pick it up. He plans to send it in to the DPS Crime Lab to get a ballistics' report, just in case it might have something to do with Clayton's death."

"After all this time...? It's been over six months!" I muttered. She was right. It was a shocking oversight. How could all three agencies, the Apache Sheriff's Department, the Navajo Tribal Police, and the FBI have overlooked that? I was puzzled. And how could Kramer not see it when he painted? For that matter, how could Bobbie Jo not have seen it when she cleaned? Surely she had cleaned before now.

"Then today," she continued, her voice unable to hide her excitement, "you won't believe what I found while going through the old files."

It struck me as odd that Kramer and his daughter hadn't gone through the files before now. Kramer was in such a hurry to open the safe, but didn't go through the files? "Go on, Bobbie Jo," I encouraged, unable to contain my curiosity.

"A Restraining Order!" she blurted. "According to the date at the top of the page, it was issued a short time after Clayton purchased the trading post."

"Against whom?" I choked on the words. She was right, it was a shocking discovery. But not quite as shocking as the person whose name appeared on the document.

A Restraining Order had been issued by the tribal police in Window Rock on Clayton's behalf to none other than our illustrious deputy, John Morgan.

Why would Clayton go to Window Rock and file a Restraining Order against Deputy Morgan? One thing I knew for sure, Clayton never liked to make waves. It had to have been a pretty serious situation for him to take such an action. I suddenly remembered that Clayton had not been quite himself at Christmas. He must have been deathly afraid, but concluding his transaction with Kramer forced his return to the trading post.

Had Morgan also made a pact with the devil? Was he responsible for my brother's murder? Or was Kramer? Were the *Chindi* using both of them? There's no predicting how, why, or when another human being might mutate before our eyes...or behind our back. All are capable of irrational behavior.

Two days later, I had returned from the Cornflower Corner's Post Office with a copy of the public document in hand. "Just what couldn't Morgan understand about this?" I asked Mother, holding the Restraining Order in my hand. "It seems pretty clear to me. According to this document, at least the way I interpret it, he was prohibited from even walking onto my brother's property. How could he be in charge of the investigation of Clayton's brutal homicide, a crime that he himself might have had a motive for committing?"

I couldn't wait to tell that badge-wearing swine what I thought of him. I didn't have to wait long. Unexpectedly, I heard his "snort-like" grunt outside my door.

"I'll get it, Mother!" I sprang up and darted toward the door.

When I confronted him with my newly found information, John Morgan was passive and failed to respond.

"Yes, a Restraining Order," I bravely repeated, in a voice of calm accusation. "And you didn't see any conflict in that?" I asked, sarcastically and maybe foolishly.

"No!" he answered decisively. "I didn't, but I might have committed an error in judgment," he admitted grudgingly.

"Oh, I think it goes beyond that!" I slammed him back. "You knew exactly what you were doing, at every precise moment. Imagine an officer who deliberately mishandles the case from the start." I chose my words carefully. "Who ignores or destroys most of the crucial clues, who blatantly disregards the law, and who should be charged not only with the suppression and destruction of key evidence, but also quite possibly with murder. You knew you'd be assigned to this case," I accused, my voice rising. "I can't believe that you accepted it, especially when Clayton had a Restraining Order against you. That paper was supposed to protect him from you."

There was no acknowledgement. He neither confessed nor denied the allegations or improprieties.

"I doubt that the sheriff would approve of such activity," I snapped.

Again, he did not reply.

"Well, I can assure you," I said in frustration. "If you don't notify your superiors of this matter, I will."

Keeping my promise, I contacted the FBI the first thing the next morning. After listening to my stream of criticism, they bent to my desires and removed Morgan from the case. But even with the seriousness of the allegations, the department didn't seem to be concerned. Apparently, I was the only person feeling horrified by what I considered to be a disgraceful, sinister sham. Eventually the sheriff's office did see to it that Morgan was transferred to another geographical location. That might have been done to avoid a first class scandal. Or, was the action simply a smokescreen to further protect an existing cover-up? These were shocking discoveries to me. Who would the Apache County Sheriff's Office send out next? Whoever it was couldn't be as contemptible as Morgan. But then again, I could be wrong, I thought.

The two new officers who replaced Morgan spoke continuously for thirty minutes straight. Using words like analyze, examine, determine, profile, and speculate, they described trails of violence and tragedy, all recited in cold commonplace tones.

Honing in on all the subtle non-verbal cues, I felt I was watching a comedy; for although educated, they perfectly embodied the characters in the Keystone Kops. Casually dressed, each wore his own individualized style of the traditional cowboy hat, boots, vests, blue jeans, large turquoise bolos, and big silver belt buckles. They were not like any of the cops I had been dealing with. After settling down on my sofa in Phoenix, the officer who had introduced himself as Mike turned to me and said, "I'm the brains of the outfit, and skinny Bobby here, is the brawn."

"We're missing something here," Bobby said. "Maybe Conway was killed due to anger."

"The killing was not an act of passion," said Mike. "It was planned in every detail by a person who is cold, who is calculating, and who has the skills and expertise to carry out such a crime. It was not done out of sudden anger. It may have been revenge."

Bobby held up his hands to interrupt Mike. "We're in agreement about everything so far, but I'd like your reasons for saying it was not done out of anger but for revenge."

"I'm not saying anger wasn't a factor," Mike said, "but it wasn't the primary motive. When someone kills for revenge, there's usually a lot of daydreaming going on along with the planning. Visions of retribution, of torture, a full hour of having the victim handcuffed to a chair while you tell him how bad he's been and what you're going to do to him, how long it will take and how much it will hurt. There has to be at least that much pleasure in it if you kill out of revenge. No one who kills out of anger kills the way this one was done—with a quick shot to the back of the head. It doesn't figure."

"Okay," Bobby said, "but I'm not overlooking anger."

"Neither am I, Bobby. But this killing, I suspect, was about fear, money, or revenge. Either Conway was threatening to expose the killer or was standing in his way, preventing him from getting something someone wanted that was worth a great deal of money."

They both agreed that Clayton's killing was one of the most grisly murders they'd seen in the reservation's recent history. Only a few clues existed, so they were left with a puzzling mystery, no suspects, and a growing list of people seeking answers to something inexplicable.

"This case really does scare me," Bobby said. "Whoever did this is extremely violent, and I'd hate to think he could do it again, but we just don't know."

I stressed that they review Clayton's Restraining Order, which I had given to the FBI.

Bobby said, "Okay, we'll check it out."

"This is just bizarre," Mike said. "One thing I can tell you, this is not a robbery gone bad. There has to be more to it. I hate to say it, but I don't think it's a coincidence that he filed a complaint saying his life was being threatened, and then he turned up dead."

Even though they didn't have any definitive answers, I liked them. They had a kind of a homespun candor. However, in the end, they didn't do anything either. In fact, it didn't take long before I began to question the validity of their information. For instance, one of the first suspects they interrogated was a person nicknamed "Juggler." At first, they told me he had an alibi during the time in question; that he had actually punched-in on a time card; that they had verified this fact with his employer. Later, they contradicted that statement, saying he was in jail at the time. Not too long after that, the very same suspect, identifying himself by his given name, approached me while I was at Cornflower Corners. He told me he was living in Hawaii at the time of Clayton's murder, further insisting that I must have had him confused with someone else when I referred to him as "Juggler."

If he was the "kid" who was with Clayton, he surely didn't look like any of the composite drawings, but then again, none of the drawings looked alike. They varied anywhere from dark skin and mustache, to dark skin, high cheekbones and no mustache, to pale, thin, and undernourished.

Unfortunately, in the dark year that followed, Clayton's death remained nothing more than a statistic. Our family experienced a bleak Christmas without him. Although we exchanged some gifts and made an effort to sing songs, our hearts weren't in it. Clayton's favorite chair at the corner of the table remained empty. During dinner, we talked about Clayton's favorite things, including music. Mother mentioned that he had been a fan of Natalie Cole, so we played her hit song, "Unforgettable" and raised our wine glasses toward the empty chair.

I had declined any social engagements that might fall on Jan. 10, the anniversary of his murder. I knew it would be a tough day. I solemnly drank my coffee and read the newspaper in the kitchen. My mind drifted back over the dismal facts of the investigation.

Although having expressed a renewed interest, it wasn't long before the FBI backed out of the case. In my opinion, they had no plausible justification in referring it back to the Apache County Sheriff's Office. I remember when they blandly told me that the FBI would be returning all documents to them.

I guess I just underestimated the formidable bureaucratic inertia of the FBI. But it wasn't just them, I realized, as I watched in helpless frustration as every law enforcement department actively involved in this case was referred back to Apache County. However, citing their legal jurisdiction, the Apache County Sheriff's Office had refused further assistance from any of these other cooperating agencies.

Why? I kept asking myself. Why, when a Payson high-ranking law enforcement official later wanted to examine the files, did they deny him access? There were still too many unexplained circumstances in this case. I could spend the rest of my life asking why, or maybe I could work harder to find some answers.

I looked ruefully at the cardboard box of files about the case that I had been keeping. Maybe if I could just sit down and document the events, things might become more obvious. I put the files on the kitchen table and started to place them in chronological order. Then I began writing about those first shocking days when Clayton's truck was found in Phoenix and the early detective reports. For the next few days, I felt driven to create some clarity from this collection of notes and papers. I wanted to make them fit together like a puzzle that would reveal the true picture. I scribbled notes on legal-sized yellow tablets. I dreaded re-reading the impersonal reports and could not bear to review the autopsy results. Mother urged me to stop dwelling on those dark times and even took me out to lunch. It became harder and harder to finish this project. One day, I was so depressed, I just put the whole box away in a dark closet.

It seemed that, for all practical purposes, the case had remained unsolved and put on the back burner. I slid into a calm acceptance. Then, one evening, as I was lying on my recliner, I switched the channel to a television show called "Unsolved Mysteries." A world-renowned psychic, Nadia Kasarian, described not only how a murder was committed, but also who had done it. She was very impressive...not an amateur, but a professional. I grabbed a piece of paper and scribbled down her name, wondering if she might be able to help us. I was desperate, and sensed, if anyone could provide assistance, Nadia had that ability.

The following week, I was able to recruit her. I discovered that she had worked with police departments before, appearing many times on "Unsolved Mysteries."

I called the Apache County Sheriff's office and spoke to Mike. "I've called in a psychic to help," I said. There was a moment of silence, then some questions. I was pleasantly surprised when he talked to other officials and they agreed to participate in a conference call. They even offered their office so more people could be included. Nadia requested some personal items. They agreed to send photos, and the hat that Clayton had been wearing when he was murdered.

That night, while I tossed and turned, unable to sleep, I tried to anticipate how Nadia would receive information. Would it be from symbols or communication from those now in spirit form in another dimension? As I lay restless, I felt my brain waves actively alternating between deep relaxation and an alert physically active state. Suddenly, I heard the phone, glanced at my bedside clock, and realized it was after midnight.

I answered the phone in a stiffly polite tone. Instinctively, I knew there was something terribly wrong with this call. As the caller started to talk, I heard a man's deep voice and began to shudder.

"If you know what's good for you, you had better get off the case," the low, mean voice warned. "This is no joke. You had better mind your own business."

"I think this *is* my business," I started to say, when he abruptly smashed the phone down, making my ear hurt. Although I didn't get to ask him, "or else, what?" I had the feeling I already knew. I considered reporting the call, but didn't want to wake Mike, since I would be seeing him the next day.

I awakened refreshed, in spite of having had only four hours of sleep, but it was good sleep, a deep sleep of total oblivion. How could things look so different the next morning? Well, today is the big event, I reminded myself, as I leaped out of bed, enjoying the adrenaline rush and wondering what kind of arcane messages the psychic would receive. More importantly, would she be able to interpret them? That was the question. At first, I was just going to wear a sweater, but knowing how unpredictable the weather could be in Chinle, where the sheriff's office was located, I decided to take my jacket.

I figured Mother and I would enjoy some company on the eight-hour drive to the reservation, especially after that threatening phone call, which I had decided to keep private so she wouldn't worry. A few days ago, my friend and neighbor had reluctantly agreed to accompany me to the meeting, where we would listen to a lady over the phone attempting to interpret cryptic symbols while in a self-induced trance.

The conference call, a method by which Nadia planned to conduct this so-called remote-viewing session, was scheduled to take place at 10 a.m. at the Apache County Sheriff's Office. For the most part, I felt that the Keystone Kops were just patronizing me. But, even the most diehard skeptics felt compelled to attend. We had no sooner arrived than Bobby, one of the Keystone Kops, motioned me over to his car. "Would you like to take a tour of our town?" he asked proudly. Not in this lifetime, I thought, as I shook my head in a negative manner and went inside.

While waiting as Nadia prepared herself, six of us sat in silence at the huge conference table.

"The universe is not just complicated; it's dangerous. There are bad things out there," Nadia cautioned, beginning to tune into "the universal mind." Her voice had a serious tone. "Any time you reach out beyond consciousness, you need to ask the Supreme Being for protection," she told us. And presumably she was doing just that, I thought, hearing nothing but silence.

Skeptical, one of the officers who happened to be standing nearby began to jeer. "You don't have to be a psychic to know this is going to be a complete waste of time," he said mockingly. Apparently, Nadia overheard him and became offended.

"Let me ask you, sir," her voice boomed over the speakerphone. "Is it any more far-fetched to believe in a universal cosmic mind, than to believe that there are other intelligent beings inhabiting millions of planets in the galaxies? Why is it so inconceivable to comprehend that there is a possible connection between our intellect and the Infinite? Does it seem any less credulous than the fact that immense dinosaurs roamed the entire earth at one time?"

"Wow, she certainly can flare up when she wants to!" The officer laughed self-consciously.

Finally, Bobby asked, "Do you believe it was some sort of a conspiracy?" Suddenly, we were all plunging into this experience headlong as Mike, my mother, neighbor, friend, and I all listened.

"Although you may think so, I do not accept that there is only one person responsible. No, the killer did not act alone. I am convinced that several people were involved," she responded. "In opening my channels, I open the third eye," Nadia said. "What I see is a scheme. A plot to kill."

As Nadia spoke, Bobby raised the still-unanswered question of how many people knew that Clayton would be up there that weekend.

"The killers did," she told us. "The killers knew he was bringing equipment from his other business. There is a younger person. A male." She paused. "Perhaps in his late teens or early twenties. In my mind's eye, I see the letter 'J,' a tattoo, I think, perhaps on his wrist…and another identifying mark on his chest."

That mental image triggered a thought in the mind of Mike, who instantly stood up. "I believe our first suspect fits that description," he said, looking over at his partner, Bobby, with a raised eyebrow. "I'll go get the file."

The energy in the room changed to one of excitement and hope. However, it brought the session to an abrupt end as Nadia said, "I hope this information is helpful."

"Yes, it seems so. Thanks!" replied Bobby.

I stood watching Mike, who hurried down the hall toward us, clutching a folder in his muscular arm, with his other arm swinging freely. I could see why everyone dubbed them the Keystone Kops. It was something in the way they moved.

Upon opening the retrieved file, Mike showed us a photo with the letter "J" tattooed on someone's wrist. In another shot, a dragon tattoo was splashed across the man's chest.

"Excuse me, where's his face?" my neighbor asked, while looking at both pictures.

"I don't know!" said Mike. "It's not in the file. Must be in another one." He shrugged it off, hoping that she would too, but he misjudged my inquisitive Cornflower Corners neighbor.

"Why would it be in another file?" she persisted. "*This* is his file. It has his name on it. Here, look," she pointed.

"What is his name?" I interrupted.

"He goes by a nickname, 'Juggler'," said the officer.

I remained expressionless, internally shocked. That was the name of a former suspect. "Why don't you have his full name on the file?" I asked.

Mike answered, "That was the only name our informant gave to us at the time."

We drove home with more questions that we initially had, stopping only to grab a bite to eat at our favorite café in Payson. By that time, we were all exhausted and welcomed a jolt of coffee.

I had hoped the new information would spur the deputies into action. They had assured me that they had every intention of pursuing the case, but these were just empty promises. I still find it difficult to understand why this information was just dropped. It seemed that everything they did or said was a charade. I wondered if I would ever know who killed my brother. Perhaps then, I could look into the murderer's face and ask, "Why?"

Two months later, I was surprised to receive a Federal Express package from Nadia, which included a tape of the session with her, and a brief note saying she thought I would like to have the items that were sent to her. I opened the tissue paper and saw my brother's tan hat with the familiar logo of the Cornflower Corners Saloon. I grabbed the hat and went to hold it to my heart, but gasped when I saw the dried blood stains. I dropped it and ran, sobbing, to my bedroom. Later, I put the tape in my desk drawer and the hat in a box that I hid deep in the closet, where Mother wouldn't find it.

CHAPTER XVI

It is interesting how all things change with time. After years of commuting from Phoenix, I finally decided to take over my brother's business property in Cornflower Corners, which consisted of an RV park and commercial building. I purchased a new manufactured home and had it ground-set on the upper level of the park.

From the deck of my new home, I could see the snow-capped mountain peaks framing the golden fields of poppies on the foothills aglow in the evening sun. I watched a thin ray of sunlight beam through the hazy, intermittent clouds. I smiled, thinking how drastically my perspective on life had changed.

"A mountaintop home is something I've always wanted," I mused out loud, trying to connect the life events that had brought me to this place. "But, I never thought my lifelong dream would be realized like this." A smile crossed my lips. Living on top of a hill in Cornflower Corners wasn't exactly what I had had in mind. Nevertheless, I was content.

The sight of a switchback trail off in the distance suddenly jarred my thoughts with a powerful memory. Five years had passed since my brother's body was found, wrapped in a tarp and stuffed down an abandoned well in an outbuilding near the Blue Sage Trading Post on the Navajo Indian Reservation. I shuddered. It's still hard to believe that Clayton is no longer with us. Soon, it will be the fifth anniversary of his memorial service.

There never was an arrest in the grisly murder case because the alleged suspect was dead, supposedly killed by a self-inflicted gunshot wound to the head. Mother and I knew it was bunk. Pinning the crime on a person who was conveniently dead was preposterous and made no sense to either of us. But we remained willing to wait and see if the real truth would be discovered one day. I still vividly remembered the remote place where the tragedy occurred—the long, snake-like twisting road, the haunting vertical shadows playing tricks on the sandstone walls. My body began to tremble as I recalled the sound of the pain, misery, and despair that echoed from within, and the canyon that swallowed me in the steepness of its shadowy craw. Although Clayton was gone, the same questions remained. Who and why? I still agonized, feeling the same frustration and hopelessness.

"Well, I can't sit here all day in blissful idleness," I reprimanded myself, although I was still feeling a little melancholy. I thought a good place to start would be to write a letter to Arizona's Attorney General, asking if there was a way to re-open the case since so much evidence had been mishandled. I went to the desk drawer to get some stationery. As I pulled out the drawer, I saw an envelope titled "Taped session with Nadia" in my handwriting. I thought, now might be the time to review this tape. It would refresh my memory. Later that night, I got up the courage to listen to the tape. I heard things I had forgotten and realized that only my mother and I knew the true details of this case. I hated that all the facts were still hidden in file boxes. Clayton's story needed to be told. Then I fell into a deep sleep.

The next morning, standing beside a column on the porch, I was scarcely able to believe what I was thinking…It had been a long time since I thought about writing a book about Clayton's unsolved case and my experiences. For years, I had avoided this project, knowing that it would be painful to re-visit those dark times. My mind searched to fill in the previous silences; my body began to feel the chill in the air that settled on the ground like a cold mist. The mystery lives, I eerily thought. Yet, I felt inspired knowing that Clayton's life was about to be forever immortalized in written form. I already knew the working title, "Secrets of a Haunted

Trading Post." Why not give it a whirl? I breathed apprehensively. But so many years had lapsed, I thought. Would I be able to retrieve the facts from my fading memory bank? More importantly, was I emotionally prepared to embark on this journey? Would I have the strength to endure the torture of reliving the events?

Immediately, my mind conjured up visions of the *Chindi,* as I remembered my first visit to the trading post. I had tried to reason out what I heard and felt that night, but there just wasn't a logical explanation. Although most people deny the existence of hexes and spells, I was not convinced.

"I can think of one other person who believes in spirits," I said out loud, as I thought of the medicine man I had met on the reservation. It was during that crucial time when we first discovered that Clayton was missing. According to what the Star Gazer told me, the *Chindi voices* were emanating from the nether world of the devil and the demons—a nether world in which the dead continue to exist. The Navajos believe that when a person dies, the corpse enters the realm of an evil world and has the power to haunt the living and inflict physical and mental pain on them.

It was difficult for me to believe that evil forces could diabolically instigate violence; that there were people who were no longer in charge of their own will. Could a mere mortal have bestowed a curse upon the trading post while engaged in some evil spell, or was that a power reserved solely for the gods? My imagination begged an answer. On my deck, lost in my thoughts, I watched as darkness came over the mountain.

The ranch, as I referred to the property, was dotted with small Malibu lights. They glowed in the walkways and in my garden. I closed my eyes in quiet reverence and began to recite the Lord's Prayer. Mouthing the words "and deliver me from evil" over and over, I prayed and whispered, "Amen." I felt the warmth of arms holding me. I knew I was destined to take a second journey through the past that might hold the answers to all my questions. Silently, I asked the Spirits for guidance, shut off the lights, and made my way to bed.

The next morning, after coffee, I stood and leaned against the deck rail; the sadness quickly vanished. From that spot, I could see the hawks soaring in the breeze and making their winding descent to the valley below. Following them with my eyes, I felt a sensation of freedom. Lifting my face to the wind and tilting my head in their direction, I watched them until they were gone. Warmth glowed inside me with introspective silence. Clayton had always loved to watch the hawks soar above us when we were kids.

CHAPTER XVII

Later that day, I went into the guest bedroom, where I kept my brother's personal belongings, all packed in a wicker chest. My heart began pounding. Piecing Clayton's story together had become my life's work. I wanted my sons, Preston and Conner, just college students when Clayton died, to know about their uncle. In the chest were many of the things found at the murder site that clearly belonged to my brother and were a part of his life.

As wrenching as this was for me, I knew that I'd done the hardest thing already: I had said goodbye to the only sibling I ever had. Clayton's belt buckle that I had given him with the inscription "Bucking Bronco's," along with a few pieces of jewelry, were tucked inside, but many of the things at the murder site somehow never made it back to us—things like keys, mugs, books, and dozens of snapshots of our family.

Even Clayton's blue duffel bag had been swapped out for a dirty brown bag. During my meeting with Morgan at the trading post, I had seen that blue duffel bag with the book I had given Clayton for Christmas propped on top of it. So, I knew he'd had those with him. For a while, I scrutinized a pair of lion-head bookends that I also had given him that last Christmas, with the caption, "Doing nothing, but doing it well." It was odd that he didn't take them when he left us at Christmas. When I tried to have a friend fly me to Cornflower Corners, so I could take Clayton the bookends and other gifts, he unexplainably wasn't there to meet us.

Then, as I continued rummaging through the wicker chest, I came across a scrapbook underneath a pile of Cornflower Corners hats and T-shirts. Its edges were badly worn, but there was no doubt it was Clayton's. I felt queasy and had to put the scrapbook down. I got up and walked around the house until I felt better; then I sat down to finish the job.

When I had first packed the book, I had studied its pages. It had travel pictures, including a view of the Atlantic Ocean off the coast of Nassau. "San Diego Regatta," slanted diagonally across the next four pages, a reference to a special combination birthday and business trip that Clayton had made to California. There were pictures of his various enterprises: one showed Clayton, Mother, and me in front of the Cornflower Corners Saloon and Steakhouse captioned, "Sure wish I could get Mother and Sarah to help out up here." Another picture was of a Navajo ruin in Utah, on which Clayton had absentmindedly scrawled his own sentimental message: "This picture cost me one dollar."

It was all thoroughly like Clayton. A record of the things my brother did to make a living, interspersed with fun memories. I wanted my kids to know everything, including what my brother did throughout his life. It was exciting, somehow, to see his familiar writing, the little doodles he had made, the quickly executed scroll work and perfectly crossed T's. It was so like him to be meticulous about everything. I recalled that the files that I eventually found at the trading post had lots of errors—so unlike Clayton. Were they written by him? Or had he absentmindedly made errors? I remembered that he had seemed distracted when we saw him that last Christmas. Then I wondered if Clayton felt uneasy and had a premonition that his days were numbered. I noticed the bottom of one page, with a photo of the Blue Sage Trading Post. "Should have never made this investment," read the note next to the picture. There it was… proof that he knew that it would be his downfall. Some answers to my questions had been right there, bound in leather, and preserved for all time in Clayton's scrapbook.

I needed a break, so I padded barefoot into the kitchen to make a pot of coffee. I noticed the lights in the den were off and the TV was on. Did I leave it on? I shuddered. I sometimes felt that ghosts haunted my home. After retrieving the *Cornflower Corners Post*, I went back into the kitchen. Armed with a steaming cup of java, I sat down at the kitchen table and opened the local newspaper. "Maybe I'm not so weird after all," I commented to myself. Amused, my eyes rested on the heading in the Religion Section of the morning's paper, "Aborigine Conducts Cleansing Ceremony at Church."

Why did these types of articles always fascinate me? I gulped my coffee, reading the article at the same time. "Don't bother me now," I scolded the dogs, as their wet noses nudged me, threatening to spill my coffee. "A little self-discipline is good for you." I presumed they liked having negative attention, rather than not having any, just like some kids.

"Members of the church ask for divine intervention…purify their church with a sacred smoke ceremony…could be compared to an exorcism in Catholicism or to some Native American ceremonies…" it went on.

"Why didn't you mention anything about the actual rite?" I chastised, throwing the paper aside. "What I want to know is how to get rid of demons, or at least how to guard against them," I demanded, as if waiting for an audible response.

In the lull, my mind began to recall a conversation that I had once overheard.

I had been taking evening classes in Catholicism, one of the many religions I had studied in my quest for understanding. While I was sitting in the dimly-lit hallway of the Roman Catholic Church, waiting for my final class to begin, I overheard a priest talking to a student.

"The Virgin Mary is the most powerful weapon against Satan. Without the Virgin's help, we are absolutely powerless against evil. An exorcist must be immersed in faith in order to survive the experience, as it involves some very vile stuff. The Church rarely gets involved with the ancient Rite of Exorcism. Only with approval from the Bishop, Archbishop, or Cardinal can such a ritual be performed…" Then, he lowered his voice to a whisper.

As I listened, I realized that until then I had been unaware that the Catholic Church accepted the belief that a person can become physically possessed by an evil force; that demonic possession was not just a notion or symbolic figure of speech.

In amazement, I further discovered that the practice of exorcism dated back to at least the time of Christ, who, according to biblical accounts, exorcised devils and gave the Apostles the power to do the same. Those were just a few of the many facts I acquired by inadvertently eavesdropping. I smiled, remembering how pleased I was with my newfound knowledge. However, thinking at the same time that it all sounded like voodoo to me.

While I was having lunch, Mother walked into the kitchen. "I thought you might like some fresh melon from the garden," she said, setting a large cantaloupe on the counter. She enjoyed her small home just down the hill from me, and had adapted well to rural life after she recently moved here.

"Thank you, Mother," I said, still reading the paper.

She replied with, "Don't tell me you're reading the religion section of the newspaper? What's wrong with you?"

"Even the Bible is full of curses," I said reflectively.

Mother looked dismayed for a moment. She seemed about to say something, then changed her mind, and walked out of the kitchen. "I've got errands to run," she shouted, and shut the front door loudly.

That was unlike her. I started to follow her, but decided against it. Maybe my obsession with writing Clayton's story was upsetting to her. I spent the remainder of the day stooped over boxes, trying to find my notes.

"I know I have notations and pictures of that windmill," I said, as I stood in the vacant building that I frequently used as a storeroom. "Where could they be?" I said to myself, shaking my head in disgust. The only interesting photos that I came across were some pictures of my sons and me on a Colorado whitewater raft trip. Even as I rifled through the last batch of papers, I recognized the futility of my efforts. I finally turned over the last box and sat on it. It was hopeless.

A noise interrupted the solitude. I hope that isn't the wind, I thought. I slowed my breathing to listen as I glanced out the window at the sky. My body shuddered. It was late afternoon, yet the mountain was cloaked in darkness. The sky was black as coal.

After dinner, I retreated to my room. Sitting up in bed, bundled in my flannel pajamas, I chuckled, still thinking about the weatherman's prediction. "This sure is a far cry from the 'misty shower' he talked about," I mumbled, as I listened to the hail pellet the roof.

"At least we're safe and warm. Aren't we?" I said to the two big mutts that were curled up on their beds. Wrangler and Roper looked up at me in their trusting way, thankful to be warm, comfortable, and cozy. Someone once joked that if past lives were a reality, they would like to come back as one of my dogs, because they were always so pampered. I really couldn't blame them. I suppose reincarnation is possible because death does not have the final word; God does. It's not so difficult to believe.

After making my mental checklist, I turned off the light. I was tired, but as I closed my eyes, memories of the Colorado River raft trip began to form in my mind. I recalled Clayton's teasing me by refusing to comment on it the last time we were together at the trading post. I got a special low cost deal on the trip package. However, I never realized that it was a thirteen-day "working trip" and not one of those luxury-catered raft trips. I remember how I had carefully packed my backpack. Its contents included a tent, a pillow, sleeping bag, most of my favorite designer play clothes, every cosmetic and cream imaginable, and even a butane curling iron for my hair, just to mention a few of the items. I remembered myself strapping the old-fashioned canvas pack to my shoulders and feeling the weight of the heavy army-surplus backpack dumping me over backwards onto the ground. I must have looked like an overturned turtle as I lay there squirming on my back.

Unaccustomed to hiking and not carrying any water, I was slow in descending the steep trail of the Grand Canyon, even though earlier I was able to coerce someone in the group to carry my backpack down. Eventually, I did catch up to where the raft party convened. It never dawned on me as to why I received such a cold welcome from those people who had waited patiently for at least four hours. One of the ladies on the trip had called me a "Wuss" and ribbed me for bringing a marble-based mirror. Later that evening, I got even with her. After a marathon night of drinking "firewater" with the rest of the group, I unintentionally threw up all over her backpack. At the end of the trip, I surprisingly received an award. The group, already having voted, presented me with a little memento: a hand-painted stone, lettered with the words, "Most Improved."

Some things make a lasting impression on us and serve as a conduit for change. For someone who was acclimated to "city life" and whose worst fear was breaking a fingernail, the raft trip was one of those life-changing experiences.

Clayton admitted that he'd encouraged me to raft the Colorado River. "I'd take the whole family on this one, Sarah," Clayton had told me. "It sounds like something your kids shouldn't miss, kind of like the ballet you took them to see…"

He paused. He never needed to finish the sentence. I knew what he meant—how embarrassed I was when my kids dissolved into hysterical laughter at seeing their first pirouette. Clayton laughed almost as hard when I told him about it.

I hadn't thought of my brother in this light for so long. All I seemed to dwell on were the terrible last moments that ended his life. I had always taken for granted that he would be here and that I would always be able to see him in his trademark outfit of sweat shirt, ball cap, and jeans.

Five years later, I could still feel the explosive headache—that awful feeling I had the night my brother was shot—like a bomb had gone off inside my head. This week, the anniversary of his funeral, I felt that old familiar shudder. Even though today was just another mark on the calendar, it would always memorialize the final Farewell Day. Before the murder, I put spiritual things on the back burner. I never asked myself if I was ready to meet my Maker.

My thoughts kept me tossing and turning. As I rolled over to my side, my eyes caught Clayton's picture glowing with the reflection of the moonlight. With tears in my eyes, I reached over and held the picture to my heart. Holding his picture, I finally drifted to sleep. The sound of the phone woke me. I knew it was Mother.

"Yes, Mother," I said, without saying hello. "Come on up for coffee, but I must warn you that I've decided to finish my book."

"You've what?" she responded, in disbelief.

I repeated the statement again. "And you know what that means," I continued, leaving no room for argument or urging her to answer.

"Yes, I know," she replied. "I'd better not stay long."

While waiting for her to arrive, I dreaded discussing our upcoming visit to the cemetery. I thought of how circumstances had changed both of our lives. Back in my class-conscious days, I wouldn't have lived in a "Podunk" community like this on a bet. Now I dreaded having to make a trip to Phoenix. I think Mother was just as surprised to find that her weekly visits led into monthly visits. Now it looked like she, too, would be here permanently, living closer to me and Clayton's final resting place. My thoughts were interrupted by her footsteps.

"Well, hello! Have you been good boys?" she chirped cheerfully to the two big dogs.

She followed me into the kitchen and I poured two cups of coffee. We drank from ceramic mugs. "Ever miss the Valley?" she asked.

"No, I do not miss the Valley," I said, letting the coffee slide down my throat. It was tepid, not hot. She saw the expression on my face. "There's something wrong with that coffeepot," I explained. "Sometimes it works; sometimes it doesn't. Just another one of the weird things around here."

As we chatted, I asked her, "Do you miss the Valley?" I hoped she was enjoying this lifestyle and liked living here as much as I did. I knew it had been quite an adjustment for her. At least she's busy all day at the little gift shop, I thought, thankful that we had the foresight to build it, both for her sake and mine.

She replied, "Actually, I like our lives here. I think your brother would have wanted it this way."

I breathed a sigh of relief.

Mother was born in Manhattan and raised in upstate New York. Her family owned a boarding home in Rochester, where students from Eastman Kodak School of Music stayed. One of the students, Andrew Resnick, a violinist of Russian descent, fell in love with Clarisa Cunningham Conway. They were married in New York City. After World War II broke out, they discovered that Clarisa was expecting a child. Andrew served in the army as a Russian interpreter, and Clarisa stayed home in Rochester. Once the war was almost over, and Andrew had completed his stint in the service and returned from overseas, the couple moved to Cleveland, Ohio. Their first child was born in 1943, and they named me Sarah. Four years later, they had Clayton. The rest is history.

After drinking only one cup of coffee, Mother got up to leave.

She looked at me for a moment. "I can find something to do at the gift shop while you work on your book, but don't forget that we need to go to the cemetery this week. I'll get the flowers and candles. If you need me, you know where I am. Let's plan on Wednesday."

"That's okay with me," I replied.

"I got the strangest feeling, after reading your horoscope in the newspaper this morning," she said in a hushed voice.

"What's that?" I asked.

"Your work has paid off. And the path of your life will change."

"I don't know what that means. Is it good or bad?"

She hesitated. "Good, I think."

Suddenly, we were laughing, and neither of us really knew why. Except that maybe Mother was right. Our work had paid off and somehow the world had changed.

"I don't mean to rush you, Mother, but I am anxious to get started…" Before I could finish my sentence, she was gone.

Just before sunset on Wednesday, Mother and I drove to the small, quaint cemetery surrounded by purple mountains. The temperature was unseasonably warm, almost eighty degrees, but we sat in the shade of a pine tree on the southwestern lawn of the Cornflower Corners cemetery, where residents of the town had erected a rustic memorial composed of a three-foot arbor of flowers in the shape of a heart. Mother bent down to place a bouquet of flowers at the foot of Clayton's gravestone. Then we lit a dozen votive candles in shape of a cross. We listened to the cooing of the doves as the sun set. Soon, the only light came from the flickering candle cross.

Mother and I received some thoughtful cards from local residents, who remembered Clayton's service five years ago. We didn't see many of them on a regular basis.

After the saloon fire, Cornflower Corners had virtually become a ghost town. Fortunately, for me as well as for everyone else, a couple, both descendants of old-time pioneering families, purchased the east parcel of land where the Cornflower Corners Store once stood. Out of the ashes and rubble arose the new store, saloon, and steakhouse. Salvaging the original hand-hewn concrete block walls, they resurrected a building so resembling the original structure that today it stands almost an exact image of its earlier incarnation.

Most of my efforts concentrated on improving the west end of the property, which included renovation of the commercial complex. I had already made major improvements to the "Cornflower Corners RV Corral," justifiably renamed upon the installation of a grand wooden fence that circled its perimeter and of horse-headed columns that guarded the entrance. If only my brother could have seen me now, with shovel in hand digging in the dirt, he wouldn't recognize me. Recalling the Feragamo heels and the elegant high-fashioned clothes I used to wear, I smiled. Clayton had always wanted Mother and me to participate in his business. Wouldn't he be surprised!

Perched above the creek stood the new store that we built, The Sinagua Creek Trading Post. The western gift shop, adorned with chili pepper lights, was transformed out of an old abandoned trailer, using weathered barn wood and antique fixtures. A traditional carved Indian, wooden watering trough, and old wagon on display completed its rustic image.

Life here was so much more relaxed than the fast-paced, competitive business world in the big city of Phoenix, just one hundred miles away. I'd shed my desire for a country club status along with my designer labels. Now those things meant nothing to me. Sometimes, my socks didn't even match. How affected I used to be. Even my dog had to be named after a designer! Being called "Gucci" had to be humiliating for that eighty-five-pound Pedigree Boxer, although it did fit his regal, well-bred manner. Naming my current dogs Wrangler and Roper was an indication that I've changed a lot.

We all go through various stages in life. I used to tease Clayton about living in a place called Cornflower Corners. "What do you do? Who do you talk to? What could you possibly have in common with anyone up there?" Now my children bombarded me with the same questions. Thinking back, when I was their age, anything that smacked of rural culture was suspect. I was hopeful that someday they would understand.

One of my friends, who had recently visited from the Valley, made the comment that some of our locals looked as though they had been chewing on lead-based paint. Granted, many of them had missing teeth, but after a while, you just didn't notice. I reminded him, "The only person you have to prove anything to is yourself. What you personally achieve as an individual, as a family member, and as a member of your community is the only basis on which you can be fairly judged. They may lack teeth, but not grit. Take a good look in the mirror, glamour boy." I really socked it to him.

There's not enough time in the day, I fretted, as I climbed into my pickup with my two dogs already on board. They knew the routine and watched my every move, waiting patiently for the familiar command to "Load up."

"It's amazing how my interests have changed," I laughed, glancing in the rear view mirror at the dogs hanging over the sides of the truck. Taking them out in the desert and turning them loose on the back roads had become a daily form of recreation for them, and for me. Each day held an adventure. Sometimes, we went to the creek, where Wrangler, the big black Labrador almost mastered the art of fishing. I watched him lunge and splash in the hope that a fish would miraculously "fly" out of the water and into his mouth, and this amused me for hours. On occasion, one did! It was a trick that he later attempted to teach Roper. Other times, I just ran them alongside the truck. I always found an abundance of things to see and do. Even the scenery changed depending on the time of day.

"We don't have much time to explore today," I explained, patting their furry heads. "No, you're definitely not city dogs. There probably aren't too many dogs that can both jump and walk a cattle guard." Wrangler, the dominant male, was usually busy hiking up his leg at every bush, marking the borders of his frontier.

"Now, you boys go play with the varmints." I encouraged them. "I want to look for rocks." They understood my every command. I hoped that they didn't take that literally.

I smiled, recalling the time when I playfully ordered the dogs to "Go get a rabbit!" Sure enough, they did.

Naturally, I couldn't resist the urge to share that amusing story. Oh, no. It was too good to keep and too tempting not to tell. Before I knew it, I had told everybody.

"I never thought they'd be able to catch one," I said, bragging later that evening in the community lounge to anyone who was in range of hearing. "A wild rabbit, no less," I asserted, piquing everyone's interest as I recounted the story, elaborating as I went along.

"You should have seen Wrangler strutting down the road, his head and tail held high. He was so proud carrying this black furry rabbit locked carefully between his jaws."

My euphoria wore off quickly, however, when that last statement caught the attention of a rancher, who was sitting within earshot. I'll never forget the expression on his face as he jumped up off his stool, or my embarrassment as he yelled from across the room: "There's no such thing as a black, wild rabbit, lady! So, that's what happened to my rabbits. I got three dead and the rest are all runnin' loose," he fumed. "Those damned dogs of yours turned over every pen in the place."

I didn't blame him for taking a dim view of the matter. After thinking about it, I realized I never had seen a wild black rabbit. He clearly thought of me as an empty-headed city blonde. However, all in all, he took it pretty well. At least he didn't shoot the dog—or me, for that matter.

In the rear-view mirror after an evening walk, I could see the mountain splashed with color from the setting sun. In front of me, the dogs trotted along past the colorful spring flowers. Each dog was vying for the lead as we all happily headed toward home.

No rabbits, thank goodness!

CHAPTER XVIII

My bones ached from driving on the bumpy roads after an outing with the dogs. You'd think I'd be accustomed to it by now, I groaned upon arriving home. Immediately going over to the little corner where I'd set up my computer center, I flipped on the switch to my new computer. At least now I wouldn't have to erase and rewrite a thousand times, I thought, adjusting my position in the chair. Words began to form in my mind and flowed quickly, the same way they had done so many times before. I proceeded to write, neatly arranging my notes, and stacking the finished pages.

I worked all day and half the night, unless something important distracted me. I was becoming emotionally and mentally exhausted. One day blended into the next as minutes of sleeplessness turned into hours. Except for running the dogs, the only exercise I ever got was jumping out of bed and writing myself notes for the book. I seemed to have lost my sense of time. My sons always teased that I was obsessive and compulsive. Maybe they were right, I thought, as I raced to get my thoughts on paper.

The book had become my comfort, my passion…my release. My writing represents my life and how I have lived it, as I continue to recall important events. We all have thoughts that we transfer from our mind to something we can create with our hands. It isn't what we have or own or what profit we make that really matters. It's that we use our creativity well. Whether we use our hands to create art, music, or to pick up a small, frightened child, or comfort one who is sick. There is healing power in our hands, just as there is a force that moves the artist's brush.

I also realized that fate surprises us and leads us in directions we don't expect. I continued to feel that I was being led down a new path toward my destiny. At times, I even had the eerie feeling that I had written this book before. I double-checked to see if I wasn't repeating myself. It also seemed as though the words were coming through me and that Clayton was there with me helping me to write it.

Looking out at the sweeping view, I realized that one of the greatest pleasures of living in Cornflower Corners has been waking to the howls of coyotes, which often are heard just before dawn. Surprisingly, I have learned to distinguish the differences in their amazing array of vocalizations. If I happen to miss that wake up call, I can always depend on the neighborhood roosters to wake me. To think I used to live by the clock. Now I can't imagine wearing a business suit, carrying a briefcase, or scheduling myself on appointments all day long.

It was getting late. I was still trying to transcribe my notes. There are no "ifs, ands or buts about it"…it is tortuous work to write and edit a book. *Tortuous*—the same word my friend Melanie used frequently in describing some of my longer sentences when she proofread my work. She was right. I had a true talent for saying in one hundred words what could be said in ten. My female friendships routinely outlive my male relationships. Melanie and I go back a long way. Back, in fact, to the time when we were both pushing our babies' strollers around. As luck would have it, my dear friend Kathy also came back into my life. She made a huge difference in my book. Her input was as good as it gets!

Straining to catch the last rays of the sun that were filtering in through the west-facing window, I was anxious for the day to draw to a close. I had fixed dinner at five o'clock so that I could go to bed early. Perhaps tonight I would get some sleep. But that night, I tossed and turned restlessly, as I felt the presence of the *Chindi* again.

The next day, while sitting mindlessly at my computer, I suddenly felt myself being pulled into a world beyond, which somehow led me to the realization that I must go back to the trading post. It was time to confront the spirits that seemed to have assumed a life of their own. I wondered if Kramer and his daughter were still there, living in that timeless isolation. I had to find out. I also had to meet with the Navajos. They knew everything, but were hesitant to share their knowledge. They had eyes in the back of their heads, but were very tight lipped.

CHAPTER XIX

During the course of the murder investigation, I had made friends with Mary Ellen, a lady who worked for the local Payson Sheriff's Department. She volunteered to go with me and so did Melanie. It was my last chance to go up before the snow. As the three of us got ready to leave for the trading post, I realized that if we didn't go now, we would never make it until after the spring thaw.

For me, this was to be a quest for answers. Even though Madelyn's trip to the trading post had fallen short of her expectations, I didn't have any preconceived notions. I didn't know what to expect or what we would encounter. I just knew I was seeking the truth. Perhaps I would find it while wrapped in a blanket, meditating in a hogan. Who knows? But I knew there was no turning back now, as the three of us prepared to embark on our journey.

Melanie had packed a cooler for us and stocked it with all kinds of goodies. "Didn't I mention not to pack anything too elaborate?" I said to her, while taking a bite of a chocolate-covered strawberry, which was easily accessible in the cooler. She isn't known for her culinary talents, but this was surprisingly good. "It's obvious you've come a long way in your cooking skills since the time you first prepared cranberry sauce!" We laughed together, recalling how Clayton, after having tasted her sugar-laden home-made cranberry sauce years ago at Thanksgiving, had put a small gift-wrapped can of Ocean Spray cranberry sauce under the tree for her at Christmas.

We loaded up my truck and set out. The desert was green and lush as we traveled higher and higher. You didn't have to be a botanist to appreciate the beauty. The agave plants with their tall stalks topped with bright flowers were in bloom. Also in bloom were the Century cactus plants, which sometimes are called *decade plants*. That's about how long they live. The century plant, at the end of the ten-year cycle, suddenly sends up a fifteen-foot stalk. The giant stalk will flower magnificently for a short time before dying. When it does die, the entire plant dies. The dead stalk then falls to the ground, where the tiny miniature plants continue the cycle by rooting themselves in the soil.

The old McGinnis sign was still there. The dirt road was pockmarked, rutted, and bumpy as I turned off the paved roadway on the way to the trading post. It seemed like I was going to lose all the fillings in my teeth. I watched Melanie and Mary Ellen jiggling and listing in their seats.

"I warned you that you'd have to endure a rugged stretch to get there," I laughed, "but this is nothing compared to what's up ahead!" The road kept getting rougher. Amazingly, we traversed the primitive trail with surprising ease. Then we were into the switchbacks on the steep climb to the trading post. It was much cooler at this higher altitude. For the rest of the way, we drove with the windows rolled down, which proved to be quite scary, especially when we had to jockey back and forth to get around some closely spaced boulders that forced our high profile vehicle very close to the edge. I was certain those boulders weren't in the roadway the last time I came up here. Maybe, since then, they had been put there to keep people out.

Where is everybody? I wondered, as the three of us stood outside the silent compound. Built from the land, but not of the land, the fortress, once alive, now looked dead, its brown weathered front merging with the weathered brown of the sun-scorched earth. The gaunt blades of the windmill still shimmered in the sunlight.

Smells are powerful memory triggers. Sometimes it takes only one aroma to bring back a part of one's past in its entirety, I realized, as I inhaled the dank earth. As I stood there, ever so quietly, it seemed that I could almost hear the old trading post breathing. Then I detected the faint odor of whiskey. As we entered, I saw that the place had been trashed. There were broken cups and dishes. Rat-chewed rubble, ankle deep, covered the floor. The place was in chaos. "What in God's name happened here?" I asked. There were baby blankets and toys strewn all over the place. I kicked away an old foam mattress that was covered by a pile of discarded clothes, next to where the washer and dryer once stood. There was still a huge black-crimson blood stain on the porous concrete floor. How in the hell had all the investigative agencies missed seeing a blood stain? If they had done their jobs properly they may have determined sooner it was murder. Walking past the wall where the bullet hole had been patched and painted over, I suddenly felt a deep stab of pain. It occurred to me that while I was here, I needed to find a medicine man to conduct a Nightway Ceremony, a ceremony for healing. A few years ago, you couldn't have forced me to come back to this place. Why was I compelled to return now?

An edgy darkness engulfed the place. It seemed that if we listened carefully we might hear the ghosts of the past. I was growing a bit uneasy. Then it happened. I heard it—the pitiful voice of the demons who had been cast into outer darkness, the voice of the *Chindi*...the voices from hell, or so I thought. Apparently, the message was meant for my ears only, for no one else seemed to be affected by the spine-shivering screams.

"Let's get out of here! Now!" I said, grabbing Melanie and Mary Ellen by the arms as we ran. "Don't tell me you didn't hear that!" I stammered once we were outside. They both looked at me blankly. "We didn't hear anything," Melanie finally admitted. "But there was someone who drove a dark blue pickup truck by the front entrance at least four times."

Her words startled me. Madelyn, in her psychic vision, had cautioned that one of the vehicles involved was a red pickup truck and the other was dark blue. "I think it's time for us to find the medicine man whom I originally met five years ago. Someone around here must know where he lives on the reservation. If we can locate Camille, she will know. We can start, I suppose, by inquiring at this farm house."

It was the same one where I had stopped at on my first trip, when I was lost. Could that be the same little Indian girl? I wondered as we drove into the yard. She looked so much taller, so much older. It was her, all right, and she remembered me.

"*Yaateeh*!" She greeted us in the traditional welcoming way. Then she lowered her head. "I heard about the tragedy," she began. "Was that your brother who was killed?"

"Yes. He was my younger brother," I told her. "He was my only brother."

"I thought so," she said. "Now I know. On that day he died," she whispered softly in Navajo, "*Taa ei bijj daaztsq*. I was so sad. How can I help you?"

"We need to find Camille, the lady who worked at the trading post for many years. We think she might know how to locate the medicine man who lives somewhere on the reservation."

"*Dzil*," she said pointing to the mountain.

"You mean we have to go back up there again?"

"On the other side," she said, "there is a dry wash." She continued using the Navajo term *Chash k'eh* for dry wash. "Camille lives in the third house past it. But if you are looking for the medicine man, I know of whom you are speaking." She smiled. "He is my father."

"Can you believe it? Her father is the shaman!" I burst out, causing my friends to grin.

"Is your father here now?" I asked.

"Yes. He is in the sweathouse, *tachech*. Please come. The sweat lodge is where he purifies himself. The lodge frame is made with willow poles and completely covered with blankets," she explained. "In a fire pit, lava rocks are heated for approximately two hours. Participants enter the lodge and the first of the heated rocks are placed in the center. Cedar leaves are scattered on the rocks and a sage switch is dipped in water, which is sprinkled on the rocks, creating steam. Prayers are said and a ceremonial pipe is used. In the intense heat, my father will meditate, pray, sing, drum, and communicate with the Creator."

We followed her through a thicket of pinon pine trees along a meandering path to the backyard. "That is a beautiful skirt you are wearing," I commented.

"Thank you, *ahehee*," she responded, clearly pleased that I had noticed. "There is a sing tonight. That's why I am wearing it."

"That happens to be one of the reasons we are here," I told her. "Could you please ask your father if he can do a sing for us, a ceremony for beauty, happiness, and well-being? I need one that will heal a broken heart." I put my closed fist to my chest. She understood and nodded.

"Father, *azhe e ataa*," she said in Navajo. That was about all I could hear. She talked to him while holding up the flap door to the sweathouse.

"I will interpret for you," she said, turning back to face us. "I told him that you are the sister of the 'Indian Trader,' *naalghehe ya sidahi*. I told him it was your brother who owned the Trading Post, *naalghehe ba hooghan*, and that he was killed that night about five years ago. He already knew of it. He said he will tell you about it later, but first, he must finish his prayers in preparation for tonight. We can wait in the house if you'd like."

On the way back, she stooped and grabbed a handful of pinon nuts, placing them in her sash, a beautifully woven native belt. "Pinon tree, *cha ol*," she pointed as if she were attempting to teach us Navajo. "Juniper, *gad; gad ni eelii*," she said, encouraging us to repeat it. We all just stood there, rolling our eyes, as we shared our silent embarrassment, knowing there was no way we could pronounce the word for juniper, which became even longer when she added the word tree. It was no wonder that during World War II, no one was able to break the Navajo Code Talker's language.

Surprisingly, her home was styled in a typical middle class manner, except for the numerous dream catchers, which were placed above all the interior doors. Dream catchers are oval or round wall hangings that look like spider webs. The Native American legend tells that all dreams are caught in the Dream Catcher. Through the center hole flow your good dreams. Bad dreams are trapped in the web and disappear with the morning sun. Needless to say, I have several in my home.

She was very gracious, offering us every kind of traditional Navajo food under the sun, which by now, I noticed, was almost hidden from view. The only catch was that she made us repeat the words in Navajo. We each had a piece of jelly cake made of yucca fruit. "*Neesdog*," I said. That word was easy. Then Mary Ellen and I had a soda pop and fried bread, while Melanie sampled some specially brewed Navajo tea. "It is very good, *taa iighisii ya at eeh*," she made us repeat. And it was.

"This was so nice of you," I thanked her.

"You're welcome, *t aa ako*," she said.

"The shaman, *hataalii*, is running late. Perhaps you can come back tomorrow. He will have more time then. I will fix some blue corn pancakes, *tse ast ei dootlizhigii*, for breakfast, if you can come early."

"Please don't go to the bother," I tried to dissuade her, but she insisted.

"Before you leave, I have something for you." She handed Melanie and Mary Ellen each an abalone shell necklace. "This one will be yours." She turned to me. "You are the sign of the rainbow. From you come all the animals." She gave me a necklace, strung with turquoise beads and adorned with animal fetishes. In the center was a dangling carved bear, framed with bear claws and teeth. "Bear, *shash*; *dzilgoo ndaakaaigii*," she said.

Overcome with emotion, I couldn't speak.

"*A yoi adeiniini*," she said.

"Translation, please?"

"We loved him, your younger brother, *atsili*."

"Thank you." I hugged her. "Now, you've made me cry." I blinked back the tears.

"That was certainly thoughtful of her, wasn't it?" Mary Ellen said, as we got into the truck.

"It was almost awkward," Melanie responded. "I didn't know what to say. I wish we could have given her something in return."

"But that's what made it so special," I said. "She didn't want anything in return."

"Let's try to find Camille," I suggested, infused with new energy. "Now that it's been over five years, she might be more inclined to talk to us, even though I realize there's no statute of limitations on what is considered taboo. She can't live too far from here," I decided, as we drove out the back entrance to the trading post. "After all, she walked home. Remember?" I reminded my friends of that fateful weekend when Camille had forgotten her keys...

"Why don't you stop there and ask?" Mary Ellen encouraged as we pulled into a driveway surrounded by a cluster of homes. "I'm sure everyone knows everybody in this little area."

Immediately, a Navajo man approached us. "Could you tell us where Camille lives?" I asked. "We are trying to locate the lady who used to work at the trading post."

"She lives over there, just around the bend," he pointed. That doesn't tell us much, I thought, as I tried to extract more information. "Can you be a little more specific?" I pried.

"She lives in the third house on the hill past the dry wash," he responded.

"What color is the house?" I politely asked.

"Gray," he said, "but she's not home," he added quickly.

"Did you get the impression that he wasn't being very accommodating?" I commented, as we drove on our way.

"He wasn't very friendly either," Mary Ellen observed.

As we rounded the bend, we could see four homes. Sandwiched in the middle was a small gray, one-room adobe. "I wonder if this is where Camille lives," I said, as I parked the truck in front of it. "Surely, she wouldn't be living up there," I glanced at the large home on the hill that was also gray. Just then, we saw the same man who had given us the directions pull into the neighboring driveway.

"Do you get the feeling that they're overly concerned about our being here?" Melanie nodded her head, alerting me to the fact that a man was approaching our truck.

From out of the two-story gray block house on the hill strode a huge middle-aged Navajo man. "It's almost like he was waiting for us to arrive."

"Exactly!" Melanie concurred.

"There are too many weird occurrences happening up here," she said, as she watched the same blue pickup drive by again. "Remember, Sarah, we're asking questions about a murder. I hope you realize we are treading in a dangerous area and need to be very cautious. We probably need to keep a somewhat low profile," she warned me and Mary Ellen.

"And this may be one of those times." Mary Ellen sunk down low in the truck seat. "I think they're having a powwow right now to decide what to do with us," she said, as she observed the Indian who gave us directions slink into the house below. "Next, we'll probably find ourselves surrounded," she half joked, reinforcing our fears.

"You've been watching too many westerns," I laughed half-heartedly.

"Wow! Will you look at that belt buckle," Mary Ellen nudged me. "It's a good thing it isn't raining. With the weight of that buckle, if he slipped in a puddle, he'd drown."

"Be nice. You're not working at the sheriff's station." I knew what she meant. We laughed.

"He acts like he was expecting us," Melanie whispered.

I assumed she was referring to the way he was dressed. He wore an immaculate starched white shirt. Displayed around his waist was the most incredible belt buckle I'd ever seen. To complete his ensemble, he wore ostrich boots and a black felt cowboy hat that was trimmed with a concho hatband. "He's definitely not a sheepherder." We all agreed.

"Can I help you?" he asked.

"Yes. We are looking for Camille. Do you know where she lives?"

He pointed. "She lives up there."

"No way," I thought, as I looked at the large, well-built, fairly new house on the hill.

"I am her eldest son. Perhaps I can assist you."

"I'm sorry," I apologized as I introduced myself.

"Of course, I remember Clayton," he said.

He seemed friendly enough, I thought, as I began to explain why we were here. "I was hopeful that Camille might be able to shed some light on what happened that night, especially since she was the last person to have seen my brother."

"I'm sure she would be more than willing to help you. But she's not home."

"Do you know where I might find her?" I continued.

"She's at work. She won't be home for another couple of hours."

I believed every word he said, but nothing could have been further from the truth.

"Do you think we can make it to where she works and still have time to meet with her before she leaves?"

"You'll have plenty of time," he smiled.

He seemed so sincere, genuinely concerned about where I lived and how I was doing. He even asked how business was at the Cornflower Corners Bar. Without realizing it, I told him everything he wanted to know about me. I told him I lived in Cornflower Corners with two big dogs. When I mentioned that the Cornflower Corners Store had burned to the ground, he didn't act a bit surprised.

"If you go now, you can catch Camille," he ended, patting my shoulder and giving me a hug. "The place where she works is only about five miles down the road. It's called the Tomahawk Trading Post," he volunteered.

That name rang a bell. Now I remembered. Morgan had told me he was at the Tomahawk Trading Post the night of Clayton's murder, on an emergency call. That also was the name of the trading post where Clayton had purchased the equipment he had been hauling that weekend; the same equipment that Morgan later claimed had been illegally sold to Clayton and that he had advised me to give back. My only recourse, he informed me, was to file a civil law suit against the Indians who sold it to my brother. Like a dummy, I just gave Morgan the equipment. He probably kept it.

What a busy place, I thought, as I looked at all the trucks parked in the trading post lot. Ah, yes. It was the second day of the month. The day that the Indians cashed their government checks. That explained it. As I waited in line, I looked around the room. "I'm not sure that I would recognize Camille if I was standing next to her," I whispered to Melanie and Mary Ellen.

"*Yaateeh*," the cashier greeted me.

"I am looking for Camille. Is she here?"

"No! She's always off on Saturday and Sunday," was her reply.

I was stunned. "Are you sure? Was she here at all today? Her son said she was working here today. Where could she be?" I continued to inquire.

"She must be at home. She usually tells us if she makes other plans."

I was floored. "Can you believe this?" I turned to Melanie and Mary Ellen. "Her son sent us on a wild goose chase."

"We know. We overheard. Saturdays and Sundays are her days off."

"I think we've been purposely duped."

I believed Mary Ellen's assessment of the situation was correct. It was a stalling tactic. By sending us on a wild goose chase, it gave them time to decide what to do with us. Perhaps they had to call another party to make that determination. Whatever it was, none of us were about to go back to confront him.

"Do you think they're trying to cover something up?" Melanie said. "Could they have had something more sinister in mind?"

"Either way, it's a scary thought. I know that Camille's relatives Lenny and Wilbur weren't exactly fond of Clayton after he fired them, especially since they had worked at the trading post for almost thirteen years. Camille did admit, however, that the only thing her cousins ever did all day was to stand around and look out the window…and drink whiskey."

"Look at the size of the house she lives in. It's pretty new. Where did she get that kind of money?" Mary Ellen commented.

"Maybe it was a payoff to keep quiet."

"Or maybe Camille was involved." Mary Ellen retorted. "Wasn't there some confusion regarding the key and wasn't it Lenny and Wilbur who found Clayton?"

"Or maybe her son was just mistaken," Melanie countered. "I don't know, but I know I'm not going back to her house. You two can save that trip for another time."

We had gone only five miles when I discovered that one of my tires was flat. The warm active fear I had felt the moment before turned now to cold numbing terror as I wondered if the *Chindi* had anything to do with it. At least it didn't happen while we were heading down the hill.

"Have either of you had any experience in changing a tire?" I inquired. Mary Ellen had, but not in the dark, she informed me. Now what? "Would you ladies prefer to walk back to that little farm house where the medicine man lives or camp in the truck?" I was concerned about spending the night in the high desert with the coyotes, scorpions, and rattlesnakes, but felt confident that the three of us could handle the situation.

"At this point, I really don't have a preference," Melanie said. "I'm just plain tired. I'll get some firewood so we can build a fire."

"I guess that means we're staying the night. The two of us can sleep across the seats in the extended cab," I said to Melanie, "and Mary Ellen, you can take the covered back bed of the truck if you want." My younger son had always poked fun at my little affordable Dodge, saying he always wondered what kind of person would drive this kind of truck. Occasionally, it came in handy.

Huddled around the fire on a pitch-black night, the exhilaration gone, we tossed pinon shells into the burning pit. We discussed everything from the Dark Ages to cosmic collisions, which according to Mary Ellen were upon us.

I finally got the opportunity to tell one of my stories of when the old timers in Cornflower Corners used to make pure corn whiskey. "The way I hear it told," I began, as Mary Ellen and Melanie laughed, "some ears of corn were put in the corn cribs for the chickens. The rest, including the stalks that were dried and cut, were blown into a silo. The weight of the corn naturally forced all the juice to the bottom. The heat created in the process caused it to ferment. Voila! Moonshine! According to my source, you could get drunk just from the smell of it. The same with Apple Jack juice…"

"You do have some interesting stories," Melanie exclaimed. "Tell us more." She laughed again.

I told them all about the Apaches gathering acorns under the shade of the ancient oak trees and about how they used to live in Sinagua Basin among the settlers. I reminded them of the earlier inhabitants of the Basin, the Sinagua Indians, who used to live in caves, pit houses, and cliff dwellings."

"I was really looking forward to this trip," Mary Ellen said enthusiastically. "This is a great diversion. It makes me forget about things like taxes and the news."

I mentioned what I had learned about the various desert plants and their amazing ability to conserve water. "The mesquite tree gets all the water it needs. It sends a taproot from thirty to one hundred feet down to find an underground source. But how does the small seedling survive the long dry spell until its taproot hits water? That's just one of the unsolved mysteries of the desert. The saguaro, as you know, starts out tiny but ends up a giant. By the end of its first year, the seedling may measure only one-fourth inch. It reaches one foot tall after fifteen years, seven feet after fifty. Its first arm comes at age seventy-five. When mature, a saguaro cactus produces tens of thousands of seeds a year, some forty million in a lifetime, only one of which may survive into old age. It may live up to two hundred years, with a trunk two and a half feet in diameter, be fifty feet tall, and weigh ten tons, four-fifths of which is water. After a rainfall, these green giants may soak up two hundred gallons of water, enough to last the saguaro a year.

"And those pretty annuals that bloom in the spring and carpet the desert floor, actually have special chemical inhibitors within them that prevent them from sprouting unless enough rain has fallen to soak the ground sufficiently to see them through their complete life cycle."

"You're just a fount of knowledge," Mary Ellen teased.

I proceeded to explain how the Ancients used resin from creosote bush to repair broken pottery or as pitch for baskets. Globe mallow flowers were chewed to relieve hoarseness. Mesquite was used for black paint to decorate pottery. The leaves of the yucca plant supplied the bristles for a paintbrush.

Energized by being in bear and mountain lion country, and feeling somewhat fearful, I even told them the odd but true tale of Leo the Lion, the famous MGM lion who was the mascot that opened many of that motion picture studio's movies. "In September of 1927, the four-hundred-pound lion was being transported in a small plane from California to New York. The plane crashed in a mountain range close to Payson. Leo and the pilot both survived. It's a true story."

"I think I've had enough tales of the Wild West," Melanie said. "I'm going to sleep."

"Sounds like a good idea to me," Mary Ellen agreed.

The following day, in spite of having had to fix the flat tire, we arrived bright and early at the shaman's house, just in time for blue corn pancakes. To my surprise, they were quite good—not dry or grainy, in spite of being made from corn meal.

While we were sitting in a hogan, smelling the sweet scent of incense, the medicine man told me, "My purpose is to free the flow within you so that you can work this out. The powers of the mind are within you. You will soon understand the unexplained." There was something in his eyes that sent chills down my spine. As if he knew what still lay in store for me.

The shaman seemed to be the wisest person I'd ever known. He, with the aid of his daughter, conducted the ceremony. When I was first saw him that morning, he was wearing an elegant blue velveteen tunic and a belt of silver and turquoise. However, by the time the ceremony commenced, he wore only a towel and a headband that held back his gray shoulder-length hair. He was the embodiment of a universal Guru emanating wisdom beyond his sixty years.

The group consisted of an unusual blend of people: a young, blonde girl, singing traditional Lakota songs; two gentlemen from Europe, who were uniquely versed in Sanskrit Mantras; and several members of the Navajo tribe, who chanted in their native language. All of them were eventually clad in only T-shirts or towels, including my friends, Melanie, Mary Ellen, and me.

Nothing had ever seemed more sacred, the blessings, the prayers, the intense chanting that continued deep into the night. At first, I only felt heat, but then I sensed a presence, but saw only fleeting images folding into shadows. It wasn't until the shaman waved his feathery wand through the steamy smoke that the visions became unveiled, whirling into the mists, swirling faster and faster. Outside, the increasingly rapid beat of the drum perpetuated the illusion. The shaman blessed all of us at the end of the ceremony. He took my hand in his and said, "Not everyone possesses the gift of 'knowing.' Trust your intuition and the answers will come to you." We drank some water and cooled down, changing into our clothes before getting into the truck. We drove home in silence.

After we returned home to Cornflower Corners, my friends and I said our farewells. I retreated to my room. I was tired, but as I closed my eyes, memories of the Sweat Lodge Ceremony began to form in my mind. I could see the small sweat lodge, made of branches and covered with skins. I tried to recall the sacred event. I envisioned the red steaming hot coals that looked like molten lava, surrounding the steaming rocks. I was relieved that my thoughts were beginning to come together as I tried to hang onto the images…Drawing in a deep breath, I winced, recalling the intense heat. My lungs ached. "I wouldn't want to go through that again," I said to myself, throwing the covers aside. As I lay there, not fully awake and yet not asleep, a weary smile crept upon my face. I knew, if given the opportunity, I would do it all over again. I hadn't really learned anything about Clayton, yet I felt something important had occurred.

The house seemed unusually quiet when I awakened the next morning. Mother had gone to the city with a friend and the dogs were still sleeping.

"I wish I could remember that Prayer Stick ritual," I said to myself, as I flipped on my computer. Unfortunately, all I could remember were parts of the blessing, of facing the four directions, each with its own sacred significance and inhaling smoke from the sage bundle as the shaman blessed me by wafting the aromatic smoke toward me with an eagle feather.

Suddenly, the phone rang. It was loud and shrill. I picked it up on the first ring. It was Bobbie Jo. I hadn't talked with her in a long time. The last I knew, she was no longer at the trading post and had opened her own wholesale operation. She wanted to know if we needed any merchandise for our store. Her husband, a well-known Native American artisan, frequently supplied our little gift shop with unique custom-made jewelry. "Sure, Bobbie Jo. Come on over tomorrow. I should be down at the store around ten."

The next morning, while waiting for Bobbie Jo and her husband to arrive, I sat on the deck beside the life-like cigar store Indian. He looked so real that one time I actually overheard an elderly customer asking him for directions.

They arrived promptly. The day was already becoming uncomfortably warm, but at least the huge overhanging roof that covered the deck provided us shade.

While looking through their display cases of jewelry, I couldn't help but admire a hand-sawed bracelet. "What a magnificent creation," I said, looking at the eagle and turtle fetishes.

"Thank you," Bobbie Jo's husband said. He proceeded to tell me an Indian story:

"The turtle was crossing a river and complained, 'The water is just too swift.'

'Hold on to this string,' the eagle encouraged. 'I will ferry you across…

'I wonder who made that lovely nest in the sand,' the eagle said, looking down as they were crossing the river.

The turtle couldn't resist opening his mouth and saying, 'I did,' and let go of the string."

Just then, and without even a glance in our direction, a coyote sprinted past us.

"I bet that little rascal saw us," I said to Bobbie Jo's husband, whose given name in Navajo was Coyote.

"I'm sure he did," he grinned. "Coyotes are very intelligent. They can outsmart most of their adversaries. Ancient Indian myth says 'brother coyote' will be the last animal alive on earth, a prophecy that wouldn't surprise many hunters or ranchers. In Native American mythology he is part god, part animal, part human, and is known as the Trickster. He'll take on any form necessary to win, and though frequently killed, he always comes back. One day, when we have more time, I would be happy to tell you more of our stories and parables."

After I purchased several items of jewelry and a few Kachinas, we were about to conclude our business, when Bobbie Jo brought up that heart-wrenching time during and after Clayton's murder. As we talked, she told me that she and her husband had ended up operating the trading post for a short time after her dad decided to go back into construction. Although I had heard of his decision, I never got a satisfactory explanation as to why Jerome Kramer chose hard labor over managing the trading post. I knew that Bobbie Jo and her husband were no longer living there, but it threw me for a loop when they told me why. Her husband first gave me some background on the Navajo philosophy about death before continuing with the weird details of their experience.

"I believe the trading post is haunted by the living dead," he told me. "The first week when we found ourselves alone, I heard these sounds. Bobbie Jo couldn't hear them, but I did. However, I am Indian. It's not unusual for Indians to have psychic abilities," he continued.

"Strange occurrences would happen in the evening, more and more frequently. At that point, I talked to a medicine man who resides on the reservation."

"There is a spirit that does not rest," he told me. "Not Clayton's. The medicine man made that very clear. And not Morgan's kid either. Their spirits are at peace."

"Then whose?" I asked, shocked, as I felt both fascination and fear.

"A baby's," he said. "The medicine man told me there have been three murders. The first murder was that of a baby, a half-breed, killed by his own father's hand. Then there was Morgan's kid and Clayton."

I was unable to muster anything more impressive than a hoarse gasp. "How can that be? Whose baby?" I choked. Far back in my mind, something like a huge piece of a jigsaw puzzle fell into place. I thought about what the Star Gazer told me that time I was up at the trading post searching for clues. The words rang in my ears, "My baby is dead; my baby is dead. You've killed my baby." Did Morgan have some connection in the baby's death? Could that have been Morgan's baby? If so, he was even more despicable than I thought. A rampage of questions whirled through my mind. My gut sensed it was true. I had been convinced that Kramer had made some sort of pact with the devil—the *Chindi*. The question—a scary one—that begged to be asked was whether Morgan had also made a pact with the same evil, restless spirit. Worse yet, was his son mistakenly killed for Morgan's past mortal sins? I began to confide in Bobbie Jo's husband about my first night at the trading post, when I heard those horrible cries emanating from some mysterious entity and my subsequent trip when I heard them again.

"I know; I heard the same thing. According to what the medicine man told me, it was the baby's voice that we heard crying and screaming its blood curdling wails. It was trying to warn us about the *Chindi*. It was trying to warn us to get out. The trading post is cursed," he continued. "It is cursed by the dead souls who are out there doing the devil's bidding. It is cursed by the *Chindi*," he said, pronouncing the word with a short "e" sound. "The devil incarnate, the devil himself."

"It forced us to leave," Bobbie Jo interrupted.

"What do you mean by 'forced' you?" I felt the goose bumps on my arms.

"Wait until you hear the rest of the story. Then you'll know…and keep in mind that my husband doesn't drink alcohol."

"We were no match for the unseen evil spirit," he added. "It was like it knew what we were planning to do next. I had recently purchased a brand new four-wheel drive truck. It was morning. Bobbie Jo and I were heading down the big hill. Who'd ever think that the brakes would go out? But they did. I flipped the truck end over end, crashing and bouncing off the sidewalls of the canyon. While this was happening, a shadowy feeling stirred within me. I can't explain it now, nor could I explain it when the auto repair shop found the brakes to be in perfect working condition upon checking them after the accident. I think the *Chindi* tried to kill us. That was enough of a warning for me. We moved to another state."

"Before I leave, I want to give you something," Bobbie Jo smiled. "My husband made it for you. You are the sign of the rainbow," she said. "From you come all the animals." Imagine my shock when she placed the dangling-bear fetish necklace around my neck. My hair stood on end, as if I had been hit with a bolt of lightning. I was speechless. The necklace was identical to the one given me by the Indian girl!

After Bobbie Jo and her husband left, I thought about the unexplainable aberration in the brake's mechanical workings and how unusual phenomena seem to occur when, for no earthly reason, albeit non-life threatening, my computer jams and sinisterly deletes pages of my book.

The next night I stayed up late, trying to finish the final chapter of my book. Upon reflection, this was quite a scary story I was writing. It wasn't at all like the make-believe ones I used to tell my children, where in the end a brave child could always conquer whatever monsters were out there; where there was always a moral, always an escape route; where good always triumphed over evil. Unlike my stories, this one had no ending. I was left with the same questions that had plagued me right from the start. Who had killed my brother, and why?

As I looked out through the window with the natural moonlight streaming in, I settled into a meditative state, thinking about the spiritual consequences of sin and the search for justice. I was quick to condemn. First, I criticized John Morgan. Why he failed to turn over evidence that could have possibly led us to a suspect would now remain between him and his conscience. I always suspected there was more to the story. Careful in my attempt to separate fact from allegation, I stopped short of pointing an accusing finger at him—a guilty conscience needs no accuser.

Mother said that an odd feeling gripped her when Morgan first asked her, "What's your gut reaction about what happened to Clayton?" It seemed as though he wanted to see what she knew.

Clayton had told us that the previous owner, who turned out to be Morgan, was pleased to be out of the trading post business. Later Morgan came to me claiming that Clayton still owed him $10,000 on the transfer of the lease for the trading post; however, he didn't have any documentation to support his allegation. Unfortunately, that was not unusual. Many people came forward claiming verbal agreements once Clayton was gone.

Several questions continued to plague me: Why did Morgan allow Kramer to immediately paint the area inside and around the crime scene while it was enclosed with yellow plastic tape with the words "Crime Scene: Do Not Cross" printed on it? In my opinion, Kramer should have been arrested for Criminal Trespass for violating and contaminating a crime scene. However, the department never pressed any charges.

Shortly thereafter, I had been notified that Kramer's young daughter, Bobbie Jo, had found a huge dried, ground-in blackish blood stain on the concrete floor in front of the washer and dryer where the killer had apparently wrapped and dragged Clayton's body in an effort to dispose of it. At first, not realizing it was blood, she began to clean it up. It wasn't until she found a bath towel in the dryer that matched the one in the freezer that she made the connection. She concluded that, at the time of Clayton's murder, both towels were in the dryer. The murderer must have reached into the dryer to take out one of the towels in order to wipe up the blood. If there was a question that any other evidence had been overlooked, it was a moot issue now.

With no evidence left to test, I was sure we would never get a conviction, even if we did have a concrete suspect. The way Morgan had manipulated the crime scene and destroyed physical evidence, he should have been charged with gross misconduct, conflict of interest, dereliction of duty, obstruction of justice, or something, especially considering the restraining order that had been issued against him. But the officials in the Apache County Sheriff's Office appeared unfazed.

John Morgan, I remembered, was very concerned about the telephone activity that took place around the time of Clayton's disappearance. Yet, when I asked him if anyone had ever followed up on tracing the phone numbers that had previously been in the FBI's possession, he admitted that no one had. His excuse was that they didn't have the manpower. I was skeptical. Surely, between both agencies they had enough staff to call a handful of numbers. Curiously, when I asked for the files containing those numbers, the page that included the time frame just prior to and after Clayton's murder was missing. With all this in mind and considering all that had happened, I wrote letters to both the State Attorney General and the Apache County Prosecutor, asking for an internal investigation. I also asked permission to copy some documents for my files. But I never received a reply.

I know that the kid who was with Clayton could not have acted alone. In the first place, he wouldn't have known that I was actively involved in the case. He was long gone. Whoever called and threatened me knew that I was the one responsible for getting the FBI and the psychics to enter the case. It had to have been someone from the inside who called me. I remember how Morgan seemed edgy when I first brought in the FBI. He didn't expect it.

The scheme's success also depended on delay, which was accomplished by inaccurately reporting when the truck was abandoned. Whoever placed that call almost had to have been involved. In his statement to the Phoenix police, the anonymous caller indicated that the truck was parked in the same spot the day before. It couldn't have been if both Madelyn and the person who saw Clayton's truck in Payson were correct.

Jerome Kramer had become an easy scapegoat, especially since he stood to gain financially. He had been asked to take a polygraph test, but he refused. It was the prevailing opinion, however, that Kramer was involved, either directly or peripherally. According to the sheriff's office, everyone knew that he had a rap sheet a mile long. I began to think that there might have been a link between Kramer and Morgan, and maybe even Richard, the guy the cops affectionately referred to as the "good ol' boy," even though he stole all of Clayton's money. However, when Bobbie Jo told me that Kramer carried a .357 magnum around with him for months, even to go to the bathroom, my suspicions of him waned, but not entirely. Perhaps Bobbie Jo said that just to throw suspicion off her dad.

Early in the investigation, I was surprised when I found out that Sue's son had been brought in for interrogation. It wasn't the first time he'd been questioned either. He'd had previous brushes with the law. Later I learned, mostly through hearsay, that Sue, the manager of the bar, and her husband had some kind of quarrel with Clayton just before he left for the trading post. A neighbor, who claimed that Sue's husband was brandishing threats, overheard the fight.

At one point in the investigation, a local resident came forward as a witness. He informed the police that he could identify the person who was with Clayton, describing him as having a tattoo on his wrist that looked like the initial "L." Could that have been the letter J, only backwards? Nobody followed up on that lead either.

Reality finally sunk in. It was apparent that nobody was ever going to do anything. At least I felt some relief that I no longer had to live under the shadow of someone's threats. Or did I? I wondered, as I watched the two horned owls that had taken up residence in the RV Park. According to Navajo belief, the owl signifies wisdom; however, under certain circumstances, the owl can serve as a messenger of impending doom. I realize that sometimes I tend to have a perception of danger which is not a reality. Yet, in other situations, I foolishly proceed where danger actually does exist and warrants caution.

For the next full week, I worked on my book, writing what I thought to be inconsequential bits of information about our trip to the reservation. It wasn't until the following Sunday that I realized the trip's significance.

It was late evening and I was getting ready to run the dogs. Wrangler was on the deck, but seemed nervous. It was odd that I didn't see Roper. He was usually right next to Wrangler. "Where's your buddy?" I asked. Then Wrangler and I walked over to the truck. The tailgate was closed. That seemed really odd, I thought. I never kept the tailgate closed unless I was going to town. I opened it.

"Oh, God!" I cried out.

Roper was lying motionless in the back of my pickup truck. He was barely alive and in a state of shock. Somebody had put the tailgate up, the lid down, and turned the latches, assuring that he would either suffocate or be baked alive in the back end of the closed truck. I made some frantic phone calls.

The vet, the fire department crew, and my dear friend Nancy all tried to help me save him. But our efforts were futile. He died. Thoughts of failing Roper while he was entrusted to my care brought me to my knees. Who would have wanted to hurt Roper? He was like a happy, overgrown puppy.

Then I realized that maybe this wasn't about Roper. Maybe this diabolical act was directed at me, to serve as a warning to back off. Somebody had warned me once before to get off the case. Was Roper's death just another attempt to convince me? Could the fire have been the first? That could explain why the lock to the side door of the Cornflower Corners Store was found broken. Unlike some people who believed that the lady who leased the restaurant was the culprit who started the fire, I never thought the fire was an inside job. It was just too coincidental.

However, proving that suspicion was another matter. So many suspicions, so many unanswered questions. Who was covering for whom? Was Morgan covering for his friends the Indians, or were they covering for him? Were they all in it together? Wasn't it odd that Jerome Kramer had never again set foot in the town of Cornflower Corners, the town where he was born and raised? Not to mention that, due to his previous land purchases, he once practically owned the town. I was certain they all had something to hide. Unfortunately, the murder investigation was compromised to the point that we would never know the answers. I never heard from or saw Madelyn again. I never did learn or come to understand why, despite all her dealings with my brother and her insights into his death, she had no inkling that Clayton had a sister. Nevertheless, I continued to write.

Many of the strongest taboos in Navajo society deal with death. In the old days, a funeral was a private affair with only one or two people involved in the burial of a relative. If the person died in the house, the house and everything in it would have to be burned to release the spirit. Another of their taboos is that they never slept facing north because that is the direction of evil and death.

At least I had that much going for me, I thought, as I got into my east-facing bed. As I lay there, almost asleep, I had this queasy feeling that someone or something might not want me to be writing about this case. Although I finally went to sleep, there was a place in my brain that stayed awake, listening for noises that might be serious enough to demand that I awaken.

While I was listening, I heard a voice within me. "If according to fate you are to lose your life, then so be it. However, it might just be that there is something God wants you to learn or create by getting through this experience." Was writing about it the way I was meant to deal with the tragedy that had befallen my family?

Things happen for reasons, but things aren't always what they seem. Nothing in life is a coincidence. Events and experiences, things that happen, are actually opportunities that are drawn to us.

An awful thought occurred to me. Was my brother's life sacrificed just so that I would have a chance to turn mine around?

And I have. My life has changed drastically and will never be the same.

I remember Clayton saying when our father died, "We have no guarantees against losing something that we cherish: a loved one, a pet, home, health, money or job. We can only make a choice as to how we will handle the losses."

I must recognize that in the grand scheme of life, there are just some things I cannot change. Maybe it will take me a lifetime to learn that lesson. "Telling your story is the one last thing I can do for you," I silently said to my dead brother. I must finish, but how can I finish what I do not understand? Evidently, the Curse of the *Chindi* lingers. Every morning, scenting death, Wrangler goes over to the hill where Roper is buried and pushes the dirt with nose, as if to say, "Come on! Get up! It's time to go for our run." I know he is puzzled and grieving too.

I am upset that, despite a tapestry of clues, there are no remaining files labeled "pending" in the sheriff's office. My brother's murder has not been solved because those in charge of the investigation have succeeded in "closing the case" by accusing a deceased person, who, to my knowledge, was never a suspect or involved in this case.

Official records say it's over. But a nagging voice I hear in the stillness of the night asks, "Or is it?"

ABOUT THE AUTHOR

Following her love of adventure, Sandra Fendler has traveled internationally as a former flight attendant. She also has a successful business background and has operated a variety of enterprises including a gift shop, where she bought and sold works created by Navajo artists.

The author has been an Arizona resident for forty-five years and currently resides in a small community where she enjoys nature, animals, and an outdoor lifestyle that inspires her writing. This is her first book of fiction.

www.ingramcontent.com/pod-product-compliance
Lightning Source LLC
Chambersburg PA
CBHW070007260626
47159CB00005B/1708